Sibling War

Sibling War

CRISTINA MONRO

PARTRIDGE
A Penguin Random House Company

ISBN: Softcover   978-1-4828-3212-9
             eBook   978-1-4828-3213-6

To order additional copies of this book, contact
Toll Free 800 101 2657 (Singapore)
Toll Free 1 800 81 7340 (Malaysia)
orders.singapore@partridgepublishing.com

www.partridgepublishing.com/singapore

There are two things in life for which we are never truly prepared: Twins

– Josh Billings

For my exceptional and talented grandchildren **Adrian, Bryan, Nixie, Prairie, Iñigo, Miggy,** and **Ines** that when they are old enough to read this book, they will realize that good siblings are treasured gifts from God.

Note from the Author

My personal experiences with my own siblings sparked the concept for this book, that siblings can be at war, but this is not about them in any way, and there are no similarities whatsoever.

CHAPTER 1

Birth of the Goddesses

"Two peas in a pod" does not always aptly describe twins, even identical twins for that matter. Athena and Diana are fraternal twins and are different as night and day. They can never be referred to as *"two of a kind"* either. They were born an hour apart during a sinister night dominated by successive peals of thunder and ensuing flashes of lightning. These resulted in power interruptions, which blanketed the Oakland Medical Center in San Francisco in complete darkness until the generator was switched on. Not a good omen, the twins' father, Rodrigo Bravo, thought.

The twins broke into the world with loud, feisty howls, so Rodrigo told his wife Marina that their twins are an aggressive and independently minded pair, and it would be fitting to name them after goddesses. That was how the namesakes of Athena, the Goddess of Wisdom, and Diana, the Huntress, came into being.

Athena is the older of the twins, fair, and an inch shorter than her sister Diana, who has a slightly darker

1

complexion. They are endowed with expressive brown eyes and brown hair. Since they were babies, they could not be left in the same crib by themselves. It always ended in cries of protest in a duet of infant shrieks, and they were only babies who just could not get along with each other. The people around their family, like relatives and friends, found this most unusual. They had never seen babies behaving like enemies at infancy.

The twins were a handful for mother Marina. She quit her job as secretary when they were born, and she opted to be a stay-at-home mom. It proved to be a great sacrifice on her part because of the twins' combative behavior. She found herself often picking up after them and settling infant disputes. As barely toddlers, the twins had the tendency of throwing their food at each other. It meant that Marina had to clean up the mess on their high chairs and mop the dirtied floor.

She realized that if she decided to return to her office job, no sane person would want to take over. Word had already spread in the neighborhood that the Bravo twins were difficult to handle. It was not easy to get a baby sitter when the need arose, so they had to hire two whenever she and her husband had to go somewhere without them.

Taking care of the twins daily was Marina's lot, and hers alone. She accepted her role as mother to impossible twins. She did not complain because she loved them dearly. They were very cute as babies and as toddlers, and she received countless compliments about their looks when people spot them outside the home.

From the very beginning, Rodrigo and Marina were resigned to the fact that their twins could not get along. They were aware that the twins could not even be made to sit together, so when traveling, they put them in separate baby carriages. Rodrigo attended to Athena and Marina to Diana, and sometimes they switched responsibilities. When handling their baby carriages, they never let them face each other or else the twins would start throwing their toys at each other.

Parenthood became an overwhelming reality to Rodrigo and Marina then. In the first place, they failed to comprehend why siblings could not be friends. From their own personal experiences, they did not develop any form of discord with their siblings. They were friends with their siblings, and still are. They never played favorites with their twins, and they saw to it that they treated them equally. Athena and Diana were accorded the same love and attention, and had the same toys. At times, they were compelled to ask themselves the question *"Where did we go wrong?"*. They even consulted a family therapist about it.

The couple's common wish was that their twins would outgrow their behavior as they get older, and they would eventually become friends, but the years proved that it was not meant to be.

CHAPTER 2

Growing-Up Years

The Bravos did not have any more children after the twins. They felt that their twins were enough to keep them on their toes. Coming home from work, Rodrigo tried to relieve Marina of some household chores so she could cook dinner. He had his taste of child management, which drained him of whatever energy was left in him after a grueling day at the office. He works as the retail department manager of Actus Enterprises, a manufacturing company where he and his staff are constantly kept on-the-go in the scenario of stiff market competition.

As the twins were growing up, Marina thought it was a cute idea to dress them up in identical dresses. It proved to be a bad one because the twins hated it. When they were seven years old, they were invited to a birthday party of the daughter of Marina's friend. They separately donned their dresses for the party, but when they discovered that they had identical clothes, trouble erupted.

"I'm not going to wear the same dress as hers!", Diana declared angrily.

"Neither do I!", Athena quipped.

Diana then tore the dress from her body and dumped it into the waste can. Athena silently took off her dress and handed it to Marina. Similar reactions, different solutions.

As children, every birthday was a disaster because the twins refused to have one common celebration. They could not share a party as normal twins were wont to do. They simply did not want to find themselves in the same activities, so they had separate celebrations with their own choice of guests.

In school, Athena proved to be smarter than her twin, just like the goddess she was named after. Like the Huntress, Diana was the athletic one, and she also performed well academically. Aware of the existing enmity between the twins, Rodrigo and Marina knew better than to have them in the same class. They requested the school principal to assign the twins in separate classrooms. Athena was at the top of her class and earned a number of awards for academic excellence and elocution. Diana also proved to have an above-average record in the classroom and excelled in sports, bringing home several medals. Their parents could not have been any prouder, but they were constantly bothered by their daughters' dark regard for each other.

When they were ten years old, the twins developed a crush on the same boy on the block. He was everybody's crush. Kevin was a good-looking thirteen-year-old who was acutely aware he was popular with the girls. He played the guitar in a band and was a goalie on the soccer field. He knew that the girls, including Athena and Diana, were attracted to him. During a soccer game, Diana caught him smiling at Athena, who blushed uncontrollably. Diana was disheartened with what she witnessed and decided to make her move. She crafted a note addressed to Kevin which read:

Dear Kevin,

When you smiled at me this afternoon, I realized that you like me, and I happen to like you too. I hope we can be good friends. I really want to know you better.

Love,
Athena

When Kevin received the note, he waited for Athena after school and confronted her.

"Hi, Athena Bravo. I want to be your friend too. I'll walk you home," he said in a domineering tone.

Athena was taken aback, but was at the same time tickled that he talked to her. Kevin kept in step with her as she was walking, and suddenly he took hold of her arm. He held on to her in a tight grip. She tried to wrest her arm from him because she felt that something was not right. He seemed fresh for someone she faced for the first time.

"What's the matter? Why are you trying to get away from me? I thought you like me. You said so in your note."

"What note?," she retorted. She was confused, and Kevin appeared to be as well. "I don't recall writing you a note."

"What are you saying? You sent me a note and it was signed by you!"

"I did no such thing!"

Then she quickened her pace and distanced herself from him as far as she could. This was not how she pictured a nice guy. Kevin was taking advantage of her. What a big turn-off, and her interest in him waned abruptly. It was then that she realized that someone played a trick on her. There was only one person on her mind who was capable of doing that, and her anger simmered.

CHAPTER 3

Womanhood

The Bravo twins, by which they are popularly identified in school and by their friends, passed their tumultuous teens of constant rivalry, but they did not outgrow it as their parents wished. They remain cold towards each other. Everyone in their young crowd knows that the twins are not good friends in any way. One cannot say that they are competing because they are gifted differently and excel in unrelated fields. Athena is an excellent writer and became the editor of the school paper in high school, as well as the champion of the debating society, while Diana was the captain of the women's basketball team and the school's star player in tennis competitions. They both have outstanding academic records.

Both women are attractive and are never short of admirers. Athena is the fair beauty, exuding gentleness and feminine grace with long flowing brown hair. Diana is the riveting dusky version with an imposing presence and brown bob hair. They are tall and slim and deserve a second glance because they are both lookers in their own right, but they do not appear anything alike. In fact, someone new in the area will not be able to guess that they are indeed twins.

On relationships, Diana is more impulsive and has had a few boyfriends even before Athena had one. Athena is rather careful in getting romantically involved because she is more inclined to focus on her studies. She belongs to a mixed study group where two of its male members obviously show interest in her and want to get close to her, but she does not reciprocate their attention.

In College, the twins are not enroled in the same university, to the relief of their parents, who believe that the distance between them may give all of them a sense of peace. Both girls are smart enough to win separate college scholarships, and their parents are thankful, knowing that a college education can be a drain on the pocket.

Athena has her first real boyfriend in college while on her third year in her Bachelor's degree in Communication Studies in San Francisco State University. She meets Philip Mann during a university lecture. He is pursuing his Master's degree and is three years her senior. Athena finds him attractive and intelligent. They see each other constantly and become sweethearts after three months of dating. It is a happy period for Athena, and she shares her joy with mom Marina.

Diana is enrolled in International Business in University of San Francisco. She is known to change boyfriends easily. She is more of the partying kind than Athena, making the rounds in socials and earning the reputation of being an elusive bachelorette who happens to be a good catch. She continues to have a string of suitors to her name because of her looks and fame, so men want to be associated with her and pursue her. Somehow she seems to be just enjoying herself with no Mr. Right in mind.

CHAPTER 4

Betrayal

The twins move in different circles. They develop friendships in school which form their respective social networks. Diana is in a gang of strong-willed women, much like her, who are popular on campus. Most of them are involved in sports and are regular spectators of sports events as a group. Athena does not belong to any gang, but she has a special kinship with Barbara Sy, a Chinese student who shares her interests in books, films, and fashion, aside from her other casual acquaintances in school. Barbara has a Hispanic boyfriend, Angelo, and sometimes they go out on a foursome with Athena and Philip.

In one of their dinner dates as a foursome in a quiet and quaint eatery, the peace is momentarily disturbed by the arrival of a rowdy group of women. Athena steals a glance and notices that one of them is Diana. She hurriedly looks away and whispers to Barbara.

"The tall one in orange is my twin sister."

By this time, Barbara knows of the sibling rivalry. Without Athena knowing it, Diana spots them and gives Philip the look-over. She knows nothing about this man, and he behaves like he has a special relationship with Athena. *Hmm, he is good-looking*, she muses.

The relationship of Athena and Philip is platonic in nature. From the very start of their relationship, she was honest with him and confessed that she is not ready to be sexually intimate. He said he understood and promised that he would wait until she is. However, she succumbed to kissing and hugging, but never beyond these. She loves Philip dearly and sees him as a future partner. They are obviously compatible. They enjoy their moments of togetherness in between their study schedules and school commitments.

Diana has other ideas. Her mind is working, fuelled by her dislike of Athena, goaded by the urge to dampen her happiness, and tinged by the embers of jealousy. She researches on Philip and learns about his personal schedule. For an entire week, she plots her move to pursue her mission. She unearths a common ground: Tennis. Diana discovers that Philip plays tennis regularly at a particular court. She figures that Athena often does not accompany him. She appears at the tennis court early, racquet in hand, and in her skimpiest tennis outfit. She befriends the guys who are there and practices with her shots. The guys are more than willing to hit some balls with an attractive female.

When Philip arrives, she pretends that she needs tennis coaching. She introduces herself to him, using the name Donna, and asks him to play a set with her, and he obliges. She does not exhibit her natural tennis prowess and allows Philip to win three of the games in the set. She knows that it is an ego-booster to let the man win. After their match, she lures him into a friendly talk.

"I'll buy you beer. You deserve it as the winner. How about it?," she tries to sound convincing.

Philip hesitates and replies, "You don't have to do that. You played equally well and could have easily beaten me. I don't deserve a reward." He is poised to leave and starts to grab his bag and racquet, ready to go, but Diana is not about to give up.

"C'mon, please," she pleads with him. "I want a beer too. It will make me feel better after my painful loss," she sweet-talks him.

That does it for Philip, and he relents to Diana's invitation. She knows exactly where to go and directs him to a bar not far from the tennis court. She engages him in conversation which centers on tennis, a topic she is also familiar with, and wins Philip's undivided attention. They discuss Wimbledon and the U.S. Open animatedly, and Philip is engrossed in the conversation. She makes sure that he downs at least three bottles of beer, just enough to keep him sober. When she observes that he is slightly tipsy, she touches his hand, making a rubbing motion, and he does not pull his hand away. That is Diana's signal. She asks for the bill and pays the waiter.

"Let's go somewhere," she whispers into his ear, and Philip does not protest.

She leads him outside. She intends to take him to the motel next to the bar. As they are making their way, Barbara and Angelo happen to be cruising along in his car, and she notices Philip.

"Hey, there's Philip," she says to Angelo.

Barbara somehow hesitates in calling out to him. As they pass the pair, she takes a look at his companion and recognizes Athena's sister with him. *Why is Philip with Athena's twin sister*, she wonders. She asks Angelo to park the car along the street, and they wait to see where the pair is going. The two enter the motel.

"Oh, no! I don't believe this." Barbara is aghast.

Diana has no difficulty seducing Philip. She lost her virginity some years ago, and she is experienced in the art of lovemaking. Inside the motel room, she immediately disrobes in front of an aroused Philip and helps him out of his clothes. He willingly allows her to guide him into the throes of pleasure. They spend the night at the motel.

The following day, Barbara takes her friend aside and relates what she saw to a shocked Athena. Athena cannot believe that Philip would betray her, and that it was with her own sister. She cries more for the hurt it inflicted on her soul than on the rage she feels. She decides to confront Philip during their scheduled date that very day. She does not want to lose any time.

"Did you sleep with my twin sister?" she questions him across the table the minute they sit down, and the direct question catches him by surprise.

"What are you talking about? I did nothing of the sort!" he denies vehemently, wide-eyed and flushed.

"Please don't lie to me, Philip. Someone saw you entering the motel with her." His face turns ashen.

"What? Are you telling me that Donna is your twin sister? That's not possible. She isn't anything like you."

"So you're admitting you slept with her. Yes, that was my twin sister, and she even had the nerve to change her name. She tricked you into it. That makes you a weakling, Philip!"

"How was I to know? She got me drunk. I'm very sorry, Athena. I didn't mean to hurt you. It wasn't about you. I promise with all my heart it won't ever happen again. Please forgive me, Athena, please," he pleads to a stony Athena.

"I won't wait for it to happen again, Philip. This ends our relationship."

"Athena, please don't be harsh with me. It wasn't entirely my fault. I have no feelings for your sister. You're the one I truly love. Please give me a chance."

"Whether it was my sister or not, the fact is you can't be trusted, Philip. You betrayed me. I don't want to have anything to do with you ever, so goodbye!" She stands and leaves him without waiting for a reply.

———————

There is still another person to confront. Athena walks into Diana's bedroom. Diana is working at her laptop, and gets up as Athena enters.

"How dare you sleep with my boyfriend! What were you trying to prove?" Athena asks her point-blank.

"That I can have any man I want?" Diana replies nonchalantly. "Your boyfriend obviously enjoyed himself with me. Ask him who's the better lover."

"I know you did it to spite me. You're an evil person. You can have him, and you deserve each other!"

Athena leaves in a huff. The betrayal is the saddest point of her existence. She has never been hurt as deeply before. For several days she grieves secretly. Only Barbara knows about it. She does not tell her mom, and at home she behaves as if nothing happened. *Why let Diana think that I'm affected.* Athena decides she will not give Diana the satisfaction.

About losing Philip, she does not care anymore. She reasons out to herself that if he can be unfaithful to her, he can be unfaithful again. She just has to close that chapter in her life. For months, Philip tries his best to win her back. He sends her letters she never bothers to read, plus flowers and chocolates, which she refuses to accept. Athena resolves to move on. She turns her full attention on her studies and reaps the reward of high grades.

Chapter 5

Employment

Graduation represents a time of jubilation. That is how it is for the twins. They are happy, in their own individual ways, that they have accomplished their goals and have earned their respective degrees. Athena graduates *magna cum laude* and Diana, *cum laude*. Rodrigo and Marina attend two separate graduations. Again, they are the proud parents, but the prevailing uncertainty and animosity cast a veil of gloom over their home. They do not know if the twins will ever be friends.

A whole new world awaits the twins, armed with their diplomas. Finding employment does not pose a problem for either of them with their glowing credentials. Companies are more than willing to hire them. They happen to be honor students, so they easily get hired by the first company they apply in. Athena joins the Corporate Communication Office of Market Strength, Inc. a leading manufacturing company, as assistant editor, while Diana is taken in as a marketing specialist by Sports Forte, a competitive and large sporting goods company.

They fit in well in their jobs, and they blend naturally into the realm of the corporate world. With their sterling performances, in barely six months, they each deserve a promotion and expectedly rise up a rung higher in the corporate ladder.

Athena and Diana are just 21 years old in their first crack at employment. Fresh out of College and greenhorns in the corporate scene mark them in their present jobs, but not for long. Soon they prove to all that they are conscientious workers, loyal to their companies, and dedicated to their positions.

Athena reports to the editor, Jane Wright, a nice and kind lady in her mid-50s who has been with the company for 25 years. Their department is Internal Communication headed by Miguel Cordova as senior manager. The company adheres to the paperless office setup, so the company newsletter their department produces is available online. They also manage the writing requirements of the other departments. Their department functions like an in-house advertising agency for these departments, which constantly need regular write-ups for their activities and internal notices that require posting online.

Diana is a perfect fit in the marketing department of her company. She is among glib-tongued go-getters, by which marketing people are known to be. Even their exchanges and repartees have a bite to them, and Diana is no neophyte to their ilk and language. She finds her place in the sun. After completing her first year with the company, her direct boss, Rupert Ryan, calls her to his office.

"Diana, we're impressed with your marketing record in the short time that you've been with us."

"Thanks for the compliment."

"How do you feel about an assignment in Europe?"

"Really? I believe that would be a good exposure for me," she replies, a degree of excitement growing inside her.

"I see that you're a graduate of International Business. Do you speak other languages?"

"As a matter of fact, I do. I also speak French and a little German," she admits confidently. "Is that going to be an advantage?"

"Definitely a big advantage. We'll work out your assignment, and I'll let you know. You'll be the right person for Sports Forte in our European branches."

"Thank you for this opportunity. I really appreciate it." Diana leaves her boss' room beaming.

CHAPTER 6

Opportunities

That night at the dinner table, Diana is excited in breaking the news to her parents about her possible posting in Europe. Athena can only listen and does not say anything, but she can feel that Diana wants envy to creep into her being in the way she delivers the news, casting a surreptitious glance at her. It sounds like a bragging right.

"Congratulations," Athena compliments her twin.

"Thank you," is all Diana can say. She cannot detect a tinge of envy from Athena, and it bothers her.

⎯⎯⎯⎯⎯

The following week, Jane talks to Athena.

"Athena, I'll be retiring at the end of the year, and I'm recommending you to take my place as editor."

"Jane, you can't retire. You're still young."

"I don't want to wait until I reach 60. My husband retired last year, and he wants us to move to a farm. It has long been a dream of his to retire in a farm. You are my choice for my replacement, Athena. You've learned the ropes and I know you can run this unit efficiently."

"This is all so sudden, Jane. I'm not sure if I'm ready to take on such a responsibility."

"You can do it. You have exceptional writing ability and you're a good editor. Accept the promotion. You deserve it."

"Thank you for considering me to replace you, Jane. I'll always be grateful to you."

"So, it's a 'yes' then. I'll tell Miguel you're accepting the promotion."

Athena is not expecting the magnitude of this promotion. She is not aiming for it since her satisfaction in her work clouds any trace of ambition to get further ahead. She believes that as long as she is happy in what she is doing, she can feel secure in her position. Besides, she is only 22, and just a year with the company. There is plenty of time to reach for the stars, so to speak.

Suddenly Athena realizes that if she will share this promotion with her parents, she will be stealing Diana's thunder. Diana has just received confirmation of her assignment to Europe, and relatives and friends have been congratulating her. *What will I do?*, Athena ponders. She battles with the issue, and her friend Barbara is a willing confidante. She is now employed in an advertising company next-door to Athena's building. They meet for lunch.

"Athena, if I were in your shoes, I wouldn't care less for taking the limelight from Diana. She's the evil sister who seduced your boyfriend. Don't you forget that!," she warns Athena.

"It just doesn't seem right, Barbs, because it's her moment, and suddenly I'll barge into her limelight.

Besides, I'm thinking of our parents. I don't want to give them any problem."

"You're such a good person, Athena. Even after what your twin did to you, you still refuse to do anything to offend her. You deserve a medal."

"It's not that. I just want to do things right." Then a thought crosses her mind.

"Diana is scheduled to leave for Europe in less than a month. Maybe I can tell our parents about the promotion after she's gone. What do you think?"

"It sounds like the practical thing to do, now that you tell me."

The twins' cousin Richard on their father's side happens to be a former College classmate of Brian, one of the writers in Athena's unit from whom he learns about her promotion to editor. He runs into Diana at a party.

"Hey, Diana, Athena is now the editor of her company, huh? I heard she was highly recommended by the editor who just retired. Congrats to your sister."

At the dinner table, Rodrigo asks Athena how she is doing in her job. She answers that she is fine, and leaves it at that, but she can sense Diana glowering at her. *She knows.*

CHAPTER 7

New Frontiers

Diana's country of assignment is France. The Sports Forte office is located in Paris. It is going to be her base, and she may also travel to other points in Europe. Prior to her departure, she practices her French everyday for two weeks with a male co-employee of French descent. He assures Diana that her French is good enough, and she will survive in Paris. He uses the word "survive" since many are aware that France is particularly not an easy country to be in for non-French speakers because the French refuse to speak English even when they know how. Diana treats it as a challenge, not as a deterrent, but she brings along with her a French-English dictionary as a just-in-case alternative despite her being sufficiently comfortable with her French.

Diana arrives in Paris at dusk on a weekend. She earlier received e-mailed instructions on how to get to the company's furnished apartment close to her workplace. Sports Forte provides living quarters for their staff who are assigned indefinitely in Paris. Diana is impressed with the place. After depositing her things at Apartment 507 of the building, she cannot wait to go down and survey the city. The city of Paris impresses her immensely, and she can see the Eiffel Tower, which at that very moment is suddenly ablaze with lights. *This is the city of love, and this is going to be my city. Paris, here I come!*

On the next working day, Diana walks to the Sports Forte office. The receptionist welcomes her and hands her an ID with her name and photo on it.

"Please proceed to Dan Jeffreys' office," she directs Diana. "It's the last door to your right," the receptionist tells her.

Diana knocks on the door, and when she hears someone inside say "come in", she turns the doorknob slowly.

"Good morning, Mr. Jeffreys. I'm Diana Bravo reporting for work."

"Of course, I know who you are. Don't call me Mister, just Dan. Welcome to Paris, Diana. I hope you find your accommodations at the staff apartment all right."

"Very much so, Mr., er Dan. I'm liking Paris already."

"Oh, you will, Diana. I can guarantee that. It's a lovely city. My secretary Annette will brief you and will introduce you to our staff. We're happy to have you with us. Rupert gave us glowing accounts of your performance. Welcome to Paris."

Annette shows Diana to her work area and gives her a folder to study about the business and how the Paris office functions. Later, she introduces Diana to the rest of the staff. Diana discovers that within the office boundaries, the language of communication is English. Their director Dan Jeffreys is American. It is when she is out in the city that she needs to practice her French.

Her first week is a familiarization period. Although it is the same company, she learns that the Paris office has unfamiliar ways of dealing with their customers. It surprises Diana, and she suspects it may have something to do with their culture. Somehow she feels that there is a lack of urgency in the way they work. They remain unruffled and seem to move with finesse. *Maybe the French do not get easily rattled*, she observes.

She finds no difficulty blending in with the marketing people, whom she joins in their after-office jaunts in classy bars and restaurants. Diana has no problem with her spending since she has no dependents, and her salary is her own. *That is the advantage of being single*, she notes, and she has no plans of getting married in the near future. She can definitely have her flings in Paris without getting seriously attached to anyone. She is going to enjoy herself to the fullest. Diana maps out the blueprint for what her life is going to be in Paris, and it thrills her.

CHAPTER 8

Challenges

Jane Wright's retirement comes to pass, and she gets honored with an appropriate send-off party. After she has made the proper hand-over of the responsibilities of the editor to her successor, it is when Athena feels that she is now on her own in running Internal Communication with the help of the five writers under her wing. She normally views work as a challenge, but with the company's forthcoming 25th anniversary, it appeared earlier to be a gargantuan challenge. She figures that to make it an appropriate celebration befitting the company's stature, they will have much to do at their end.

The company's 25th anniversary falls on the same week as her 23rd birthday. It means that she will have to forego any form of celebration of her own to give way to work. Work comes first to her at this point in her career. She meets with her staff to prepare them and to draw out their ideas. Amber, Faith, Jessica, Roy, and Brian are her hard-working writers. Athena plans to discuss first the event with Miguel and iron out details. She has a meeting with Miguel at his office that day.

"Athena, I know we're looking at our 25th anniversary as a major event for our company. Our first thought was a grand celebration," Miguel gestures with his hand to mean 'big'. "However, it was cascaded yesterday from the top to the senior managers that the event should be low-key. No fanfare. True, the company is doing well, but our CEO stressed that instead of spending grandiosely, we can channel the funds reserved for this purpose to a worthy cause instead, like helping a community. He has a point there. It's the "*Doing Well, Doing Good*" discipline at work. Do you have any thoughts on this?"

"That's sounds like a more practical way of celebrating our anniversary, Miguel. Maybe we can just put out a single ad in the newspaper to announce our anniversary to the public. Nothing ostentatious.

"Do you have anything else in mind?"

"Internally, my staff and I are thinking of creating a video on the company's history and airing it for the employees. We can also highlight it in our online company newsletter. We can organize small activities here and there, like an online trivia for employees with prizes at stake. The employees should be our main focus since they also helped the company move ahead."

"You're right there. Our employees are our important stakeholders. Which community do you think can benefit most from our assistance?"

"On the choice of a deserving community, we'll look into the list and decide which one needs our assistance the most, and find out how best we can help the residents of our chosen community," Athena explains to him.

"Surprisingly, there are several poor communities in San Francisco."

"Those are very good ideas, Athena," Miguel agrees. "Our 25th anniversary is three months away, so we have enough time to do all that. I know that our original plan centered on something grand, but now that has changed. That makes our job easier," he says with a pleased expression.

"Good for us, but no matter how conservative our anniversary celebration will turn out to be, we can still make it meaningful and significant," Athena adds.

"I like that. If there's anything you need, such as additional assistance, just let me know."

"Thanks, Miguel, but at the moment, I believe we'll manage."

Athena assigns the video to Brian, who has experience in creating one from his previous employment with an advertising agency. She farms out writing assignments to Amber, Faith, and Jessica, including the trivia. Roy handles the ad and liaises with the Art Department regarding its layout and production. She decides to interview the CEO herself to be featured in both the video and the newsletter.

Wow, the challenges are not slow in coming. She rubs on her enthusiasm to her staff, so their unit is literally humming with activity. Her biggest challenge is interviewing the CEO himself, Raoul Granger, who set up this company 25 years ago. She feels intimidated since she has never interviewed a CEO before in her life. The following week, Athena makes an appointment with Mr. Granger's secretary and explains her purpose. Three days later, Mr. Granger is available for an interview. She is glad with his immediate response.

The secretary ushers her into the CEO's office on the top floor of their building. She is overwhelmed by its sheer size because his enclave is deep and wide, and at the far end is his massive desk. Mr. Granger stands to welcome her, and she notices that he is a big man, but his physique is not threatening and belies his gentle demeanor. After just a few minutes of meeting and talking to him, Athena's earlier jitters settle down. He answers all her questions and shares with her the humble beginnings of the company. The more-than-one-hour interview she records provides her with ample details for her article.

She then drafts Mr. Granger's message to the employees for his approval. He makes only minor corrections. Brian schedules the taping of the CEO's message using a teleprompter, with Mr. Granger delivering it while seated at his desk, and Athena supervises the taping.

The company's anniversary is observed without much fuss. It is a relatively quiet and meaningful milestone. The newspaper gives the company a whole page, which chronicles its achievements. The company's External Communication issues press releases on the anniversary and the company's endeavors, highlighting its community projects. The video with Mr. Granger's inspiring message is aired to the employees, and is also featured in the online newsletter.

Athena's suggestion to focus on two aspects in their community program, which are Livelihood and Education, is approved by Miguel.

The chosen community benefits from a livelihood program, which the employees themselves monitor to give the mothers in the community a trade to master and bring in profit. They introduce a craft and search for the proper market channel for the finished products. The company provides the community with 20 electric sewing machines. The families in the community appreciate the extra income the housewives bring home because it contributes to the upliftment of their lives.

The company also sets up a tutorial service for the kids in the said community. Employee volunteers visit the community on a regular basis and help the kids with their English, Math, and Science lessons. The tutorials help the kids perform better in the classroom and expose the employees to the realities of community life.

The CEO is pleased with the outcome and sends a memo of commendation to Miguel, which he in turn passes on to Athena with his note, *"Excellent job, Athena."* It is an achievement for her and her unit, and it is an exhilarating feeling to have done an outstanding job and be acknowledged for it. Athena treats her writers to lunch as a gesture of her appreciation for their contributions.

CHAPTER 9

Independence

As Athena turns 23, she decides it is time to move out of her parents' home and get a place of her own. She can well afford it with her generous salary. She hates to leave her parents, and they are sad in seeing her go, but they understand her decision. With Diana in Europe, Athena is their only child living with them. Athena finds a newly built condominium two blocks away from her parents, and she signs up for a one-bedroom unit on the eighth floor, which has a clear view of a forested area and the ocean beyond.

This is an exciting time for her. She has a hand in choosing the colors she prefers for the rooms, and her conservative taste draws her to the warm, muted shades. She chooses a light tint of pink for her bedroom. It is not because she feels she is utterly feminine, but she read somewhere that pink is a soothing color that induces sleep. She opts for a subdued periwinkle shade for her living/dining area, and favors cream paint for her kitchen with touches of mahogany for the cabinets and moldings.

She helps supervise the carpentry work and painting to ensure that there are no mistakes committed, and even the installation of the lighting. She wants it to be a perfect place she can call her own.

Athena even has more fun in furnishing her condo, picking out the furniture pieces of her choice and hanging the curtains. Her furniture are not all brand-new, except for her appliances. She chances upon an antique shop selling reasonably priced pieces, and she purchases a few, which blend well with her interiors. When she finally moves in, she invites her parents for dinner, and they are pleased with the way she decorated the interiors. It is some sort of an accomplishment on her part.

"Our home feels so empty with you gone and Diana away. Your dad and I miss you terribly," her mom admits during dinner.

"Oh, Mom, I miss you and Dad too. You know I need to do this. I'm 23 years old and should be independent by now, and not living with my parents anymore. I'm just close by, so you'll be seeing me still, maybe even on a daily basis," she assures her parents. "Is Diana coming home soon?"

"She said by next year, and that's still a long time," her dad interjects.

"That may not be too far away," Athena says. "Dad, you can convert my old bedroom into your office and maybe a library."

"That's not a bad idea. I'll see what I can do. Your room has a number of possibilities, Athena."

"It's your decision what you want to do with it, Dad"

"Maybe an office, and I can work from home when the time comes for me to retire."

"Just perfect for you then."

"Remember, Athena, you're welcome at home anytime. Your bed is still there. It can also serve as a day bed, so you can still use it if you want to."

"Thanks, Dad. If you and Mom need anything, anything at all, I'm just a stone's throw away. The reason I picked this location is because it's close to you, and I can visit you often."

"You are always free to come to the house if you don't feel like cooking, and have a meal with us, dear," Marina offers.

"Thanks, Mom. I'll certainly miss your cooking. I'm practicing with my cooking now, and it's not anything like yours yet."

"In time, dear. Just keep practicing. As they say, practice makes perfect," Marina encourages her. "Your pot roast was good, and I had a second helping."

"Thanks, Mom."

CHAPTER 10

Connections

After working at the Sports Forte Paris office for several months, Diana cannot help but notice a strikingly attractive gentleman who definitely looks like a manager by his overall appearance. He happens to drop by Dan's office one fine morning. He is not easy to ignore with his French good looks. He has wind-blown blond hair, expressive hazel eyes, of medium height, and is impeccably dressed. The first time Diana laid eyes on him, he stared back at her appreciatively with a twinkle in his eyes. She knew then that he finds her attractive. Diana always notices when she holds a man's interest captive. The first thing Diana does the next time he visits their department is ask Marie, one of the ladies in Marketing, about him.

"Hey, Marie, who's that gorgeous blond guy talking to Dan?"

"Oh, that's Pierre Montand of Finance."

"Is he married?"

"No," Marie says emphatically. "He's a certified bachelor, the unmarrying kind," stressing the adjective. "You Americans call it 'playing the field', no?"

Diana's interest is piqued, especially after knowing that he is single and unattached.

"He's looking this way. Diana, I think he's interested in you," Marie tells her.

"No way," she answers and looks away, pretending not to notice. She returns to her desk and starts rummaging through the pile of papers on top of it. She feigns being busy with work.

Just then Dan and Pierre walk towards Diana's direction and stop in front of her desk.

"Diana, I want you to meet Pierre Montand. Pierre, Diana Bravo, our new executive in Marketing from the U.S. She speaks French."

As Diana extends her hand to acknowledge the introduction, Pierre brings it to his lips and kisses it lightly. The gesture takes Diana by surprise since no man has ever done that to her before. She is instantly touched by his chivalry. Pierre's eyes never leaves her face while doing this.

"*Enchante, Mademoiselle Diana,*" Pierre says with a captivating smile.

"*Bonjour,*" Diana responds.

From then on, he pursues her in a gallant manner. Diana is obviously flattered. Practically all the women in the office have a big crush on Pierre, but he has eyes only for Diana and starts calling her everyday. At the start of the day when her phone at her desk rings, she knows for certain it is Pierre to greet her a good morning. He is her most persistent admirer so far. One afternoon while she is busy doing market computations at her desk, she gets startled as someone whispers into her ear.

"Will you have dinner with me tonight, *mademoiselle*?" It is Pierre, who else. How can she refuse when he drops by personally just to invite her?

"Oh, it's you Pierre. You startled me. Yes, I'd like to have dinner with you tonight."

At dinner in a fancy restaurant along Champs-Elysees, they enjoy their banter. Pierre has an inborn wit, which Diana is drawn to, and she likes his French accent. A man's intelligence and wit count a lot to her. In the course of their conversation after their meal, she makes a comment.

"I notice that the French have a lot of influence. There's always something French. Look at French toast, French fries, French twist, and even French manicure. Where is it coming from? Are the French really that influential?"

"That's correct, but you missed the most important one."

"What's that?"

"French kiss, of course. It's also the most satisfying," he responds, eyeing Diana suggestively. "I suppose you know what I mean. Have you indulged in it?"

Diana cannot look at him and hesitates in answering his probing question.

"I'm not sure to what extent," she answers demurely, which is so unlike her.

"Do you want to explore that with me?" he asks her in his French accent, which hits her as sexy and inviting.

"Is that an invitation, Pierre?" It may sound too forward to others, but Diana is stirred by what Pierre is insinuating. She is no Athena to ignore his suggestion.

"*Que voulez-vous?* (What do you wish?) If it seems like one to you, do you accept?" His hazel eyes manifest the passion behind them as he looks at her.

She pauses for a few seconds, then answers.

"*Oi,* Pierre" with mounting excitement.

He quickly pays the bill and leads her to his cramped Porsche where they indulge in prolonged passionate kissing, French and all. It leads to groping, leaving Diana breathless. Pierre is an adept French kisser who knows exactly what areas in her to explore. Diana never feels so alive like now, so when Pierre suggests they go to his apartment, she is like putty to his suggestion, and more than willing to give vent to her rising desire.

That night she sleeps in Pierre's apartment, and subsequently becomes a regular occupant of his large bed. They share a preference for torrid and unadulterated sex. Among the men she has gone out with, Pierre is her best lover so far who can propel her to peaks of ecstasy. Pierre considers her insatiable, and he thinks he has found his match.

At work, it is hard for Diana to control herself on seeing Pierre because her memory becomes flooded with scenes of their love-making. The stolen glances between them are a give-away, and Dan notices these to his amusement. Sports Forte has nothing against inter-office relationships.

———— ∞∞∞ ————

On the other side of the globe, Athena approaches Miguel over a problem in the wording of a documentation for internal publication. She is somewhat concerned that it might disparage the competition.

"I'm not too sure myself about this, Athena. Let's ask our lawyers, Blake, Johnson, and Prentiss. I'll call Jonathan Prentiss and ask him to assist you. Miguel dials the firm's office number and asks for Prentiss.

"Hi, Jon. Miguel Cordova here. We're in a bit of a quandary about the wording of a document whether it's legally appropriate or not. If you're free now, may I send our editor over to see you to take a quick look at it? We just want to play safe."

"Sure, Miguel. I'm free at the moment."

"Thanks, Jon. Our editor is Athena Bravo. I'll ask her to see you now."

"Interesting name. Okay, Miguel, I'll expect her."

After putting down the phone, Miguel tells Athena to see him at the Concord House, which is two buildings away from them, so it is just a short walk. Athena is already expected, so she is ushered upon her arrival to Jonathan Prentiss' office on the top floor of the building, where the legal partners hold office. She is quite unprepared for the encounter since she expects this Jonathan Prentiss to be an oldish legal partner. When she meets him face-to-face, she stares at him for a few seconds. She cannot believe that he appears to be barely in his 30s, tall, dark-haired, blue-eyed, and very good-looking. He is likewise instantly attracted to Athena's beauty. He gives her a firm handshake when they introduce themselves and welcomes her in his deep baritone voice.

"How do you do, Miss Bravo."

"You're English," she comments with a hint of surprise on her face.

"Yes. Do you have any problem with that?" he answers, smiling at her.

"No, of course not," she responds quickly. "It's just that I thought the person I'm meeting is American."

"I hope you're not disappointed," he adds, still smiling.

"Not at all," Athena assures him.

He offers her the armchair and sits opposite her. Athena finds his presence intimidating. She has never met anyone this good-looking, yet she observes that there is no hint of arrogance in him, as if he is not even aware of his good looks. Then she turns to her purpose.

"May I show you the document in question?", and hands it to him.

He reads the document briefly, then makes his assessment.

"I don't seem to see any legal snag here, Miss Bravo." Before she can say anything, he adds, "May I call you Athena? Your parents must have named you after the Goddess of Wisdom," he comments with obvious amusement. He seems to be good-natured and with a ready smile in Athena's quick observation.

"That's right. Both my twin sister and I were named after Greek goddesses, Mr. Prentiss."

"It's Jon," he corrects her. "Well, I don't see why you can't go ahead and publish the document. No problem there."

"It's good to know that. Thanks for your time. I appreciate your assistance," Athena replies.

"It was my pleasure, Athena. You can call me anytime if you encounter anything that confuses you with legal terms. As your lawyers, it's the least our office can do for Market Strength."

She rises from her chair, and he gets up and leads her to the door. He gives her a warm smile, and Athena notices his perfect white teeth. *So unlike most Englishmen who are not known to have good teeth.*

"See you around" are his parting words. On the elevator, Athena ponders on his words. *He expects to see me again. He's very likable, and I do want to see him again,* she is certain. She then recounts to Miguel her encounter with Jon Prentiss.

"I expected someone much older. He seems to be very young to be a legal partner," she tells Miguel.

"Jonathan Prentiss is a brilliant lawyer. He graduated *summa cum laude* from Harvard Law School. The law firm didn't lose time in hiring him, and they're glad they did. He has been winning case after case for them. In fact, to my knowledge, he has never lost a case. They had to make him a partner after just one year because he deserved it. I've watched him defend a client in the court room, and he's really dynamic. He happens to be a bachelor, Athena," Miguel comments with a gleam in his eyes.

"Are you playing Cupid, Miguel?" she retorts with a chuckle.

Sure enough, on the following month, the Blake, Johnson, and Prentiss Law Office throws a dinner party at their corporate headquarters for selected clients. Miguel asks Athena to attend. It is an after-work affair, so they are in their corporate attire. Athena wears her beige blazer over a soft floral blouse with a matching beige short skirt and tan high heels.

When she arrives at the venue with Miguel and the other executives, Jon immediately spots her and walks towards them to say hello. She meets the older partners, Blake and Johnson. In the sit-down dinner, Athena and

Jon are at separate tables. Over coffee after dinner, Miguel senses that Jon wants to talk to Athena because he keeps glancing towards their table, so he exchanges seats with him. Athena is surprised that Jon is suddenly seated next to her.

"Did you like the food?", he asks her.

"Yes, it was excellent. Does your firm do this often?"

"On occasions to show our appreciation. How do like working with Market Strength?"

"Oh, I like it very much. It's my first job really. My superiors, like Miguel, are good to us, and the job is full of challenges." Then she continues, "You know, I confess that when I first met you, I couldn't believe you're a partner because you're very young. You must really be an exceptional lawyer to have come this far so fast."

"Thanks. I also worked very hard to arrive at this point in my career. Blake and Johnson are like fathers to me and have been my constant mentors, and I'm grateful to them." Suddenly he says, "May I invite you for coffee or dinner perhaps one of these days, if that's all right with you?"

"I'm fine with that. See you then."

Athena notices that everybody at the Blake, Johnson, and Prentiss Law Office addresses Jon as "JP" after his initials. She is already looking forward to their date. She realizes she did not have any other boyfriend after Philip because she did not want to get romantically involved after that unpleasant experience. She turned her focus on her career instead. *Can Jonathan Prentiss be the one for me?* The very thought of it infuses her with a warmth she cannot explain. He is undoubtedly a very attractive and smart gentleman. She can already feel the chemistry between them, so the possibility excites her.

CHAPTER 11

Constant Twosomes

After establishing rapport with Pierre physically, emotionally, and intellectually, Diana is enthused, and she believes she will not hanker for anything else. She is happy when she is with him because the day always ends with her needs being fulfilled. It is as if her satisfaction is Pierre's ultimate objective. He knows how to treat her as a woman, and he pampers her with attention and gifts. They can also converse for hours, and Pierre knows many interesting things about people and places. He can certainly hold her attention for hours.

Her performance in her job soars because she is totally inspired. Just the very thought of Pierre can make her light up. Her officemates are aware of the affair, and a number of ladies, who are eyeing Pierre, envy her secretly. They acknowledge Diana as an appealing woman, so they understand that men are normally drawn to her, including Pierre.

For once, Diana ponders on the possibility of marriage. She is aware that she does not want to get married yet and be tied down. She has always been a free spirit. It is the same thing with Pierre, who is a confirmed bachelor as everyone has accepted. It proves to be an ideal setup with no strings attached and no demands made on each other. Pierre is the perfect lover. Her happiness is of utmost importance to him.

This generates a significant change in Diana. She has never given anybody extra attention before, but now she is naturally driven to be nice to people, and to attend to Pierre's needs. She even learns how to cook his favorite dishes. This is the same woman who never goes near the kitchen. It is an entirely new Diana.

Outside the office, Pierre and Diana are a constant twosome. She stays more at his place than in Apartment 507. They have gone away on holidays. They share meals, stories, and jokes, and of course, the same bed. She is quick to notice that when they are out in the city, the women steal glances at Pierre. Diana concludes that it is because he is attractive. Pierre is definitely a ladies' man. She wants to tell them, "*Sorry, ladies, he belongs to me.*"

Diana notices that she has become sort of possessive and perhaps a tad worried about losing Pierre to other women, and she has never been like this before. When the time comes for her to visit the Sports Forte office in Geneva, she has her apprehensions about leaving Pierre. He is there to send her off.

"Pierre, promise me you'll behave while I'm gone?"

"Diana, *mon amour*, I'll be a good boy for you. Isn't that how you say it in America? I'll certainly miss you, but I won't fool around, so don't worry your pretty head. Maybe I should ask you to be careful with Swiss men. You are a very attractive woman, you know."

True, Pierre is also a bit worried that Diana may be seduced by a Swiss gentleman, and he knows her to be a woman of passion.

———

One day after work, Jon gives Athena a call.

"Hi, Athena. It's Jon Prentiss. Are you knocking off early today? I know it's a Monday."

"I plan to because it's an unusually dull Monday today. What's up, Jon?"

"That's good because I'd like to invite you for coffee at Starbucks just around the corner."

"I can do that. Is 4:30 okay?"

"Four thirty is fine. See you there."

Jon is already at Starbucks when Athena arrives. He stands and gives her his disarming smile the minute he sees her. He asks her about her coffee preference. She usually drinks caramel *machiatto*. He gets one for her and sets in down in front of her.

"So, how was your day? The usual question one would ask I suppose," he starts the conversation.

"Not too busy at this time. Thankfully. All that needed to be written were done. How about you?"

"Well, this morning I had to defend a client in court. It was an inheritance case. Siblings fighting over what their parents left them. Do you have any siblings, by the way?"

"I have a twin sister. We're not anything alike. We don't even look alike. How about you, do you have any brother or sister?"

"I have an older brother and an older sister. They're both married and have families of their own. I'm the youngest. We get along well, although I rarely see them because they're living in the East Coast in different states."

"That's too bad. You know, I feel I should tell you this, Jon. My twin sister and I don't get along at all since we were young. We're very different. When I was in College, she seduced my boyfriend, and I broke up with him because I couldn't tolerate infidelity."

"I'm sorry to hear that. Where is your twin sister now?"

"Her company sent her to France. She's been there for almost two years and due to come home soon. I don't really want to see her anymore. I recently left my parents' home and moved to a condo. Do you live alone?"

"Yes, I also have my own place. I value my privacy."

"I can understand that because that's also important to me. My parents were not exactly in favor of my decision, but my condo is close to their place, so I can still see them often."

"In my case, my mother is the only surviving parent because my dad passed away right after my graduation. At least he saw me graduate. Mom now lives with my sister."

"I'm sorry about your dad. He must have been very proud of you. How long have you lived in the U.S.?"

"My dad was assigned by his company in the U.S., so we moved here from England when I was 17, and I completed my studies here. My mom was pleased with the move because she's American. So I'm actually half English and half American. I was born in England, but later opted for an American citizenship and decided to practice Law here after graduation."

"By the way, Miguel said you're dynamic in the court room. It would be nice to watch and listen to you in court."

"Do you really want to? I can arrange that."

"I want to," she says with sincerity. "Your job must be pretty exciting, especially when defending a client in court. I've watched a lot of that on TV, even the long-running '*Law and Order*', and I enjoyed them."

"Well, it's not like that all the time, but I can tell you that it's a challenging job. It's a thinking job too, and one's knowledge of the law is paramount. I've always wanted to be a lawyer since I was a boy. My dad was very supportive and he encouraged me to follow my dream."

"I guess we both knew what we wanted while we were still young because I wanted to be a writer for as long as I can remember. When I was a small girl, I started writing my own stories, and my number one critic was my dad."

An hour of a lively exchange uncovers their individual characteristics, and sparks their interest in each other.

"Well, thanks for the coffee, Jon."

"My pleasure. Dinner next time?"

"We'll see." She does not make any promises.

———wwoo℗®⊗℗oovw———

Athena does not have to wait long. Friday comes, and Jon invites her to dinner. She has time to go home and change. She takes a shower and changes into a cotton dress. She told him earlier that she did not want anything formal, and a simple dinner would do. He insists on picking her up, so she gives him her address. He arrives on the dot in his small light blue Mercedes. While inside his car, they resume their animated talk from days earlier, and there is never a dull moment all through dinner.

"First, I have no ask you if you're not allergic to seafood because I have the perfect place in mind to take you if you're not," he says.

"No, I'm not. I love seafood."

"Then I'm sure you'll like this place, and we don't have to be too formal."

He takes her to a cozy restaurant close to the ocean which serves lobsters to Athena's delight. They wear bibs, eat with their hands, and thoroughly enjoy the lobster dipped in lemon-butter sauce. The following day is Saturday, so there is no hurry to get home. They linger at the restaurant talking until the number of patrons starts to dwindle.

"I've never eaten this much. That was a highly satisfying meal. Lobster is one of my favorites, and I haven't had that for a long time," she tells him.

"Me too. Let's do it again sometime. May I call you in a few days, Athena? I'm going to Atlanta this weekend to arrange a meeting with a client. I'm scheduled to return late Monday. Are you comfortable with giving me your mobile phone number or email address?"

"No problem, Jon. Here's my calling card. They're all there."

"And here's mine," handing her his card. "I'd like to know you better, Athena, if you don't mind."

"I'm fine with that. I enjoy your company. I had a wonderful time tonight. Thanks for that unforgettable lobster dinner."

"You're welcome. You'll be seeing me sooner than you think," he teases her, and she likes it.

CHAPTER 12

Discoveries

The saying *"Absence makes the heart grow fonder"* rings true for Athena because she is missing Jon. She has been careful about getting involved with a man again, but Jon seems different and undeniably attractive. He is very articulate, and she does not tire listening to his English accent, which reminds her of her favorite character, James Bond. He appears genuinely interested in her too. The thought of Jon barges into her consciousness, and she suddenly catches herself dwelling on him while she is working. Then she receives an e-mail message from him:

Hi Athena,

How are you? I keep thinking of that dinner date we had last Friday. We should do it more often. I must admit I enjoyed myself immensely. Too bad my only witness, Mr. Lobster, can't confirm that. See you soon.

Best,
Jon

Athena breaks into an audible laugh after reading his e-mail, which elicited a glance from her writers. She decides to write him a quick reply:

Hi Jon,

You made me laugh, and my writers were wondering what happened to me. I enjoyed our time together too. Have a safe trip back.

Athena

The more Athena gets to know Jon, the more she likes him. She has no idea that Jon also cannot get her out of his mind. Every time he thinks of her, a smile crosses his face. This occurs several times, and once during a board meeting, but he checked himself in the nick of time and concentrated on the issue at hand. He realizes he has never felt this way about a woman before. He had past flings, and he had met a number of attractive women in his life, but Athena is different, a rare specimen. She strikes him as a beautiful person externally, the kind of beauty that merits a second and third look of admiration. On the inside, she is kind and humble, aside from being intelligent. *A rare combination in this day and age.* He was immediately drawn to her the first time they met, and his feelings for her intensify as he becomes more familiar with her character.

As Jon returns from his trip, the first person he calls is Athena. *I miss her*, he is convinced.

"Hi, Athena. How's it going? I just arrived this afternoon."

"Oh, Jon! Everything okay?," the excitement evident in her voice.

"Mission accomplished. How are you? I hope I was missed."

"You were, Jon," she answers with a chuckle.

"By you?"

"Who else do you think?"

"I'm glad to hear that. Are you free tonight for an early and perhaps quick dinner? I want to see you." There is a hint of urgency in his voice.

"All right. Where do we meet?"

"I'll wait outside your building at 6:00."

—❧❧❧❧❧❧❧—

The minute Athena steps out of their building, she gets startled as Jon grabs her hand, while smiling down at her, and takes the lead. It is unexpected, and Jon's touch sends currents through her. Unlike the handshake, this time she feels the warm pressure of his hand on hers. They walk hand-in-hand to a nearby restaurant where he chooses a table for two in a secluded corner. They do not speak to each other until they are seated and have made their orders. Then Jon suddenly takes her hand in his and makes a long sigh.

"Athena, Athena. Do you know what you're doing to me?" He looks at her intently, and she feels like melting under his gaze.

"No, Jon. Did I do something wrong?" Her voice is shaking and her heart is fluttering.

"You have captured my heart, do you know that?" He gives her a lopsided smile, and the effect of it sends her heart pounding rapidly in her chest.

"What do you mean?" she whispers, her nervousness escalating.

"I believe I've fallen in love with you," he admits, his deep blue eyes glued on her with a soulful expression. "Now, before I make a fool of myself, let me ask how you feel towards me. I need to know, Athena," his eyes never leaving her, challenging her to reply.

Confused, Athena feels shy and avoids his eyes, but she manages a response. "I'm attracted to you, Jon," she answers nervously.

His face softens with her admission.

"I like you very much," she confesses further.

"Is that...?" He tilts his head and gives her a questioning look.

"I may be in love with you already," she interrupts him.

He reacts with a wide, happy grin.

"Gosh, you just made me a very happy man." He kisses her knuckles which makes her shiver with delight. "In that case, can we bring it to the next level? Will you be my girlfriend, Athena?"

"Yes, Jon," she responds without a moment's hesitation, glancing at his handsome face shyly.

He drives her home in his car after their meal. He keeps glancing at her with a smile on his face and occasionally grips her hand, which sends Athena's pulse racing. As they reach her condo, he gets out from the car and opens her door, then offers his hand to her. She loves the feel of his hand. He leads her towards the entrance, but before he lets go of her, he takes her into his arms in a long, tight hug, which confirms to Athena that she definitely belongs to this man. She breathes his manly scent. Then he speaks.

"May I kiss you? I've been wanting to do that since Day 1. Yes, my goddess Athena, you caught my attention the first time I met you."

She nods. In her heart, she has been anticipating his kiss too. *I thought he'd never ask.* He slowly tilts her chin so they can gaze into each other's eyes, traces the outline of her lips, then kisses her firmly on the lips. It is not a probing kiss, but she feels wonderful as he relentlessly moves his lips on hers. A tremor runs through her body as she surrenders to his lingering kiss, awakening her innermost feelings. She does not want him to stop, and she is totally lost in his kiss. Before she can enjoy it further, he releases her and caresses her cheek.

"Goodnight, my darling. Sleep well." Then he is gone.

He leaves her in a daze, and she remains rooted on where she stands. It is a time for discoveries. Two people discover that they love each other.

CHAPTER 13

Birthdays

It is Athena's 24th birthday the next day. She cannot recall telling anybody her date of birth, yet when she arrives at the office that morning, there is a bouquet of white and pink roses on her desk. She tears open the envelope. It is from Jon with a note which reads: *"Happy Birthday, Athena. Much love, Jon."*

How did he know it's my birthday, she wonders. Her phone rings and interrupts her thoughts.

"Happy Birthday, sweetheart. How are you feeling this morning?" It is Jon, her Jon. She is elated just hearing his voice.

"Thanks for the roses, Jon. I love them. How did you know it's my birthday? I don't recall telling you."

"I can be resourceful. Of course, I have to know when the person I love was born."

"You haven't even told me your birthday," she scolds him.

"I will, my love. First things first. You have to be free for me tonight."

"Where are you taking me, Jon?," her excitement increasing.

"It's a surprise."

"You're full of surprises."

"I hope you like surprises."

"I do too."

"Be ready before 7:00. I'll pick you up. Thanks for last night's kiss. I enjoyed it immensely. Bye. I love you."

"Love you too." The memory of that kiss plants a smile on Athena's face. There is something in Jon's accent which makes his declaration sweeter.

———

Without Athena's knowledge, her writers organize mid-afternoon snacks in her honor at the office. They earlier decorated the multi-purpose room with a sign declaring "*Happy Birthday, Athena*". The staff in the entire Communication Office are invited and get a treat of ice cream and cake. Her day has a good start. She looks forward to her evening with Jon.

———

Athena decides to wear something more dressy than usual for her date with Jon, although she has no inkling where he is taking her. She chooses a black shift dress, which emphasizes her slim figure, of knee length with abbreviated sleeves and a low back. She brings a shawl in case she might feel cold. It all seems so mysterious, and she is intrigued by it. When Jon sees her, his admiring eyes say it all as he compliments her profusely on how she looks and tells her how beautiful she is. Without giving her any hints, he leads an expectant Athena to the open area at the topmost level of his building where a table is laid out for two and a violinist is playing one of Henry Mancini's compositions, *"Moon River"*. The scene tugs at Athena's romantic side.

"Jon, what's this?" Her expression mirrors her appreciation.

"Happy Birthday, darling. I hope this is to your liking."

"This is so romantic, Jon. I love it," she confirms as she surveys the rooftop, which is lit with hundreds of tiny white lights.

"I'm glad you're happy with the arrangement. My secretary helped me plan it. Now, shall we eat? I'm hungry."

The waiter comes around and serves them dinner, which consists of creamed soup, green salad with vinaigrette dressing, and tenderloin steak with baked potato, which they enjoy with red wine. They have *crème broulee* for dessert. The table has a floral centerpiece with lighted candles. They dine under the stars with a rising moon.

"Jon, thank you for all the trouble you took to celebrate my birthday. Nothing can top this."

"I only want to make you happy, especially on your birthday. This is just the beginning. There's more." He stands and extends his right hand to her.

"May I have this dance, Athena Bravo?"

Athena accepts his hand and rises from her seat into his waiting arms. She feels the warmth of his body course through her own. She does not need her shawl after all. They dance to the violinist's selection of Michel Legrand compositions. He is a graceful dancer and guides her to keep in step with him. Jon's manly cologne is pleasantly intoxicating, and she loves his scent. In between his embraces, he looks deeply into her eyes, leaving Athena weak-kneed.

As the violinist plays "*What Are You Doing the Rest of Your Life*", he sings along softly, and Athena is amazed that he knows the lyrics of the song. She closes her eyes and enjoys it silently. He tells her that he likes her smell. He kisses her hair and her cheeks, then brushes his lips against hers, his hand gently caressing her back. She is shaking when he leads her back to the table, and she needs her shawl this time. Next, Jon produces a small rectangular box from his breast pocket.

"This is for you. Happy Birthday again, Athena," handing her the box.

"There's more?," she questions him, perplexed. "Jon, the roses and this dinner are more than enough."

"I hope you like it. Open it."

She slowly opens the box and inside it is a gold necklace sporting a pendant with two hearts. As Athena examines it, she sees that one heart is inscribed with "Athena" and the other one "Jon".

"This is beautiful, Jon. I don't know what to say."

"If you want to get rid of me in the future, you can just throw the other heart away," he suggests.

"That's not going to happen." she assures him with a soft look, touching his hand.

He takes the necklace from her and puts it on her neck. It is her best birthday ever, Athena concludes, and she tells Jon this. She cannot thank him enough, so when the evening is over, she rains little kisses on his face, and hugs him tightly to his satisfaction.

Jon is a loving person who openly expresses his feelings for her. Athena points this out to him.

"I had the impression that Englishmen are generally not too demonstrative when it comes to their feelings, but you're just the opposite."

"Really?" he reacts. "How do you want me, cold or warm?"

"I love you the way you are, Jon. Don't change."

When Jon calls her "darling" or "love", Athena is thrilled. She wants to address him in the same way too, but her shyness prevails. Maybe in time, she reasons out to herself. Her pillow is her sole witness because before she falls asleep, she whispers to it, *I love you, Jon, darling… very much.*

———

Back in Paris, Diana wakes up on her birthday and sees the other side of the bed empty. Pierre seems to have left early without knowing it is her birthday. She attempts to get up from bed when the door swings open. Pierre enters carrying a breakfast tray.

"Bon anniversaire, mon amour."(Happy Birthday, my love)

"Merci, Pierre, but how did you know?"

"I have my ways of finding out. You're not going to work today, okay? I'm taking you to a nice place for lunch and we'll spend the day all by ourselves. Now, eat your breakfast."

"Shouldn't we call the office to say we're not reporting for work today?"

"No need to do that. I already hinted to Dan, and he's okay with it because I secretly told him it's your birthday."

She is caught unaware. She cannot figure out how he knew it is her birthday. He serves her pancakes, scrambled egg, bacon, orange juice, and coffee. On the tray is also a single red rose in a vase. He takes a piece of bacon and feeds it to her.

"Pierre, you're spoiling me."

"You deserve to be spoiled, *mon cher*. You know, Diana, you've given me much happiness since we met."

"You've done the same for me, Pierre. *Merci*. This is a great breakfast."

"Enjoy it, then join me in the shower. Dress in something casual for the day."

They both don T-shirts and jeans. They ride top-down in Pierre's sports car to the countryside of France and have a nice lunch in one of the restaurants along the way. Pierre is familiar with the area and makes commentaries to her about the scenery. Diana never imagined that her birthday would be spent in such an unusual manner beside an attractive and delightful companion with the sexy wind-blown hair.

When they return to Paris early evening, they are still too full to have a normal dinner, and instead have cheese and bread, which they enjoy partaking with a glass of white wine in Pierre's apartment. Afterwards, while lounging on the sofa and watching television, Pierre gently grabs Diana's wrist and clasps on it a tennis bracelet with sparkling diamonds. Diana looks at it with bewilderment printed on her face, then shifts her look to Pierre.

"Pierre, this is expensive."

"Nothing is expensive for you, *mon amour. Tu es ma joie de vivre.*" (You are the love of my life).

"*Tu es mon homme*" (You are my man), she proclaims.

Diana's open admission expressed in French is enough to ignite the fire in Pierre. He rises immediately, pulls Diana to him and kisses her savagely, then he undresses her hurriedly, and makes love to her passionately right there on the living room carpet. Diana is panting with unexplained emotions after their night of love-making. To her, it is the greatest birthday she ever had, thanks to Pierre, the only man who can truly satisfy her.

The following morning, she reports for work with fulfillment evident [n her appearance. The people at the office who noted her absence ask her where she was the day before, noticing her happy countenance.

"It was my birthday," she replies with an obvious twinkle in her eyes. *What a birthday it was!*

CHAPTER 14

Assignment's End

It suddenly dawns on Diana that her assignment in Paris will come to an end soon. It is the saddest day of her life so far. The thought of leaving Paris weighs on her heavily for an entire week, and it has to do with not seeing Pierre anymore. It means only one thing, that this man has become an important person in her life. She is not sure if she loves him because she has never been in love before, but she is certain that he makes her very happy.

Diana does not have the heart to tell Pierre that her departure from Paris is imminent because she is worried she might cry. She is one person who is not easily moved to tears, so she cannot imagine herself crying. Even as a child when she and Athena had their fights, she never shed a tear. She has always been the headstrong one. Pierre found out from Dan, who just casually mentioned Diana's impending departure to him. Pierre confronts Diana.

"*Mon amour,* Diana, why didn't you tell me you're leaving soon?"

"I don't feel like leaving, Pierre, so I try not to think about it. I don't want to be away from you. "*Je veux etre avec toi*" (I want to be with you)."

"Well, you can always come back, or I can go visit you in America."

"Will you do that for me really, Pierre?"

"*Oi, mon cher.* Before you know it, I'm already there if you ask for me."

"Oh, Pierre. This is very difficult. I can't revoke my contract with Sports Forte Paris. I have to go home. Promise you won't do anything foolish when I'm no longer here?"

"Is that what's worrying you? I promise to be faithful to you. I won't even look at any other woman, *mon cheri.*"

"They're looking at you, Pierre. They're aware how great a lover you are."

Pierre laughs. "It's you I want, nobody else. Do you want me to sign a contract of fidelity?" he suggests teasingly.

"Your promise will do." She has to take his word for it.

They cannot get enough of each other, knowing that soon they will part. They spend every moment after work together having dinner or just strolling around Paris and enjoying each other's company. Diana never thought of herself as a one-man woman. Her original plan in coming to Paris was to meet many men and have the time of her life with the Frenchmen, who are known to be the amorous type. She simply wanted to have a plural enjoyment in another country. She met Pierre and he changed all that.

CHAPTER 15

Homecoming

Dan Jeffries and the Marketing people organize an after-office party for Diana at a downtown popular bar before her trip home. Dan invites Pierre as his guest. Dan announces to the Marketing people:

"Guys, Pierre Montand is our guest tonight. We want to give Diana a memorable send-off, and we know she's happy with Pierre around." Everyone laughs and acknowledges Pierre's presence.

They enjoy the evening to its fullest. They have fun eating, drinking, interacting, and dancing. Diana appreciates the office's gesture of honoring her, but at the same time sad that she is leaving.

———

At the airport on her day of departure, Diana is not in high spirits in the presence of Pierre. Sensing her mood, he lifts her chin and looks longingly into her eyes.

"Don't you forget that you are my woman, *n'est-ce pas?* (right)," he assures her.

Diana is touched by his words and gives him a nod. His assurance is her going-away present, and she wants to hold on to his promise.

———

Diana has never before missed any place or anyone, but now she misses Paris and Pierre unbearably. Her sad feeling somewhat diffuses when she sees her parents who meet her at the airport and are glad to see her.

"Welcome home, dear," her mom gushes while hugging her.

"We miss you," her dad says. "You've been away from home too long, Diana."

"Thanks, Dad and Mom. I miss you too." She feels the tears coming, and she knows it is not like her to cry, so she checks herself.

"We organized a small homecoming dinner for you at home tonight with just us and four of your friends who can join us," her mom tells her.

"That's nice of you to do that. I look forward to it."

When they get home, Diana realizes that she misses home. Nothing much has changed, except for the new throw pillows in the living room and a freshly painted kitchen. The door to Athena's room is open, and she notices that it is different.

"What happened here, Dad? Where's Athena?," she asks.

"Athena moved to her own condo, and I'm using her room now as my office."

"Oh" is Diana's only response.

The homecoming dinner goes well. Marina prepares Diana's favorite dishes, which she knows her daughter misses. There are shrieks of delight from Diana's friends upon seeing her, followed by an extended catching-up period. As usual, Diana is the center of attention with her gang. Athena drops by and welcomes Diana back. They greet each other briefly, then Athena helps their mom in the kitchen and leaves right after dinner.

When she reports for work the following day, Diana is greeted by a signage which says "*Welcome Home, Diana*". For a brief second, her mind is not on Paris and Pierre as she interacts with her Sports Forte colleagues.

CHAPTER 16

Silver Anniversary

The only time that Athena and Diana have no choice but to communicate is when their parents' 25th wedding anniversary approaches. They both acknowledge that they have great parents who stood by them all these years. They agree that their parents deserve to be honored on their silver wedding anniversary. It has been a good marriage. Since they are the only children, the two of them discuss the best way to celebrate their parents' 25th anniversary. This time they do not argue, and what one suggests is acceptable to the other.

Rodrigo and Marina are private persons who are not into the social scene, so the twins agree that they will appreciate more a gathering of family and relatives. They pool together their financial resources to give their parents a memorable anniversary. They consult each other before any decision is made.

Diana offers to engage the caterer her office usually hires to provide the food, aside from attending to the physical arrangements and décor in the social hall of their community, which they rent for the occasion at a minimal cost. Athena takes care of the video, highlighting the episodes in their parents' marriage, and the invitations to send out. It is a peaceful division of labor their parents may never believe possible.

Athena notices the positive change in Diana since her return from Paris. The week before the anniversary dinner, the twins reveal to their parents their plan for the celebration to give them ample time to be prepared for the occasion, and Rodrigo and Marina are extremely pleased that their twins are in it together. To their recollection, this is the first time in 24 years that they are doing something together, and they are actually talking to each other. Yet they are not too keen about celebrating their anniversary with a party.

"Girls, you don't have to do this," Marina reacts. "There's really no need for a celebration."

"Mom, you have nothing to worry about. We'll take care of everything," the twins assure her.

"Why all the fuss for an anniversary? We're not expecting this. Besides, I don't have anything appropriate to wear for the occasion you envision," Marina says truthfully.

"That's okay, Mom, we have this covered. We got you a nice dress for the occasion," Athena answers. "A new suit for you too, Dad."

"I can't believe you have this all planned. Your mom and I were going to celebrate our anniversary quietly with just the two of us," Rodrigo pipes in.

"You two deserve a celebration. It will just be with family and relatives since we know you don't like big crowds," Diana quips.

"We don't want you to go to all that trouble. It's just an anniversary, and we'll have more in the future," Rodrigo insists.

"Dad, that's 25 years of a happy married life. We want to celebrate it with you," Diana elaborates.

"We know that, but we don't want you to be spending for it. You can put the money instead into your savings," Marina suggests. The twins laugh.

"We have enough savings of our own and you're our only family to spend it on," Athena stresses, and Diana nods in agreement.

Rodrigo and Marina give in to their twins' plan, seeing that it is bringing them together. At least this aspect is something they have always wished for.

On the day of the anniversary, the social hall is tastefully decorated with a streamer on the wall at the rear of the room with the sign: "*Happy 25th Anniversary! Rodrigo and Marina*". Each table is decked with a bouquet of flowers with a large lighted candle in the middle. The guest list numbers 50 of purely family and relatives, people the couple is comfortable with. There are nameplates on the tables which Athena and Diana assigned earlier. They want their parents to relish and enjoy their anniversary with familiar faces.

There are no strangers in the crowd, thus none of their friends are on the guest list, only relatives. The only nonfamily members are the caterer and waiters. Two of their cousins volunteer to take a video and photos of the family affair. Another relative, who is a pianist, offers to play during the occasion, interspersed with piped-in music from their parents' era. The center of the hall is cleared for dancing.

Marina appears young and lovely in her mint green cocktail dress with a lace bodice of the same shade. The twins know that green is her favorite color. Rodrigo looks dapper in his new suit. Athena plays the role of emcee. When she announces the arrival of Rodrigo and Marina, the relatives applaud with gusto, and happiness registers on their faces.

The two buffet tables are laden with vegetable salad, dinner rolls, roast beef, *coq au vin*, breaded fish fillet, and *fettuccine alfredo*, with a tower of cream puffs and apple tarts for dessert with coffee. The waiters fill the glasses of the guests with red or white wine. After dinner, a waiter wheels in the large square anniversary cake and lights the 25 candles, which Rodrigo and Marina blow out together, and this is followed by a hearty applause from the guests.

The video documenting the couple's years together brings tears to Marina's eyes. It also shows photos of Athena and Diana in their childhood years. Somehow there are no photos of them together, and the family and relatives understand why. Athena and Diana each deliver a brief message for their parents, praising and thanking them. They attribute what they have become to their proper upbringing. Next Athena asks her parents to dance as the pianist plays "*I Only Have Eyes For You*". Rodrigo leads Marina to the center of the hall, and they dance to the rhythm of the music.

Dancing and interacting with one another continue through the night for everybody. The twins are glad that their parents are pleased with the celebration they prepared for them. For a moment, they each get to wonder if their own marriage in the future will be as enduring as their parents'.

CHAPTER 17

Downsizing

Downsizing is the trend in a number of companies as a coping mechanism in light of the US economic slump. The business climate has not been too favorable lately, and companies are trying to remain on the radar. Actus Enterprises, Rodrigo's company, is exerting considerable efforts in maintaining its competitive edge. Rodrigo and his staff are already working double time to keep their products relevant in the market, but it is still not enough. Their company is suffering from the effects of the widespread recession plus the stiff competition.

The possibility of downsizing is secretly being passed around in whispers in the cafeteria and pantry, and Rodrigo prepares himself for it. He is aware that his position is not indispensable and can be absorbed by his boss, and the company can save money by offering him early retirement.

When their CEO calls all the managers to a meeting, Rodrigo already anticipates the outcome. The atmosphere in the meeting room is somber as the managers sense impending bad news. The CEO then announces that due to the present recession the country is experiencing, their company has to let go of seven of its managers, otherwise its survival is uncertain. He explains that the decision is the result of a thorough study done by its Human Resources Department. Rodrigo's name is on the list, and he is just in his 50s.

Initially, Rodrigo feels dejected that he is going to leave the only company he has worked with for 26 years. After sharing and discussing it with Marina, they realize that it will not exactly leave them destitute because the retirement package from the company is generous. They can invest it and live on the interest. They also have some savings, and he can even work again if he wants to. The twins learn about the downsizing and without second thoughts offer their financial assistance.

"Dad, we want to assist you financially. Diana and I have no dependents to support," Athena proposes.

"No, that's not necessary, girls. We no longer have major expenses, no more mortgage to pay since we own our home. The state provides free health plan, and your mom and I also have some savings," Rodrigo divulges. "Thank God we were blessed with smart daughters like you, so we didn't spend for your College education because you both won scholarships. That's why we were able to save and put money in the bank. Now we're counting our blessings. Retirement for me is not really bad. I'm in a better position than others who are not ready for it."

"We want to help, so just let us know," Diana offers.

"Thanks for your offer. I can still work if I feel like it. Maybe I can do consultancy work and take is easy this time. We'll see. My job was really quite stressful, so

I welcome the retirement. I don't intend to completely stop working."

"Good for you, Dad," Athena comments.

"Besides, I have my small bread baking business, which I'm enjoying, and it's doing all right. Maybe it's time for your dad to rest," Marina adds. She busies herself with baking bread for the neighborhood and has been supplying a popular coffee shop in the area. Marina's bread is something the twins often crave for.

The reality of downsizing hits Athena and Diana, and it makes them realize that it can happen to anybody as it is happening to a hard-working manager like their father. It is good that they are still young and can make hay now. They believe that nothing is certain in the corporate world, so they resolve to work hard and make themselves relevant so that in the future, their superiors will think twice before letting them go when their companies resort to downsizing. The twins are relieved that their companies are not affected by the downsizing trend occurring everywhere.

Even if one is not personally affected by downsizing, it is still sad to see one's officemates getting retrenched as Rodrigo witnesses in his company. He feels fortunate that he is not in debt and is not left penniless by it.

CHAPTER 18

Unlikely Reconciliation

Even if the air has somewhat cleared between the twins, Athena does not get too close to Diana. She suspects something happened to Diana in Paris which is responsible for her transformation. She suddenly comes home a kinder and different Diana. *For how long?* All these years, Athena had to bear with Diana's sneers and smirks directed at her which she just ignored, and she never retaliated. Still, Athena is wary about trusting her completely.

Athena is thankful that she does not live with her parents anymore, so she does not have to see Diana. The next time they see each other is when they view with their parents the video and photos taken during the anniversary party. They make comments about them, but they do not directly address each other, and Athena is comfortable with that, and thinks it is for the best. When she drops by to visit her parents, she schedules it when she knows that Diana is not home. As much as possible, she tries to avoid any contact with her twin.

Athena shares these developments with Jon during one of their dates. Jon always has a sympathetic ear and exhibits genuine concern for her.

"I'm keeping Diana at arm's length because I don't know what she's capable of. Do you think I am being unsisterly?," she asks Jon.

"You know her better than I do, Athena. What exactly are you worried about?"

"All our lives she has done evil things to me, Jon. She seduced my former boyfriend Philip. She might even steal you away from me," she says with fear in her heart.

"Come here." Jon takes her hand, sits her beside him, and puts his arm around her. "That's not even a remote possibility because you're the one I love, and only you. Nobody can wrest me away from you. You better believe that," His expression is full of love for her as he looks into her eyes. He brings his lips down on hers and kisses her firmly. Athena can feel her heart bursting with love for this man.

"Oh, Jon, thank you for saying that. I feel better already. I love you, and I don't want to lose you."

"You're never ever going to lose me, understand?," he assures her, touching her chin. "I won't let that happen. We're meant for each other," he stresses, while running his palm along her long brown hair.

"Diana and I are twins, but we're very different. She always gets what she wants. She charms her way by employing sexual innuendoes, and that's not my kind of thing." She rests her head on his shoulder, his arm still wrapped around her.

"I know that of you, and that's one of the reasons I love you. You're a decent woman," he answers her convincingly.

After a few minutes, he suddenly straightens up as an idea hits him like a light-bulb moment.

"I have an idea, and you tell me if you're okay with it. If and when I meet Diana, suppose I won't tell her that I'm your boyfriend and see how she treats me. What do you think? Of course, I won't go out of my way to meet her, so that's only if and when I do. The likelihood of that may not be immediate, but who knows? Then we'll see what happens."

"That's not a bad idea," she responds with enthusiasm.

"How I wish I could introduce you to my parents, Jon," she continues. "I've been keeping our relationship secret because of Diana."

"That's okay. A secret it is for now. Just remember that my love for you is no secret. My office is aware of it." He tightens his hug.

"They do?," she reacts happily. "I'm sorry I can't be just as open in my office because my writer Brian was a classmate of my cousin Richard, who's close to Diana."

"Don't worry about it. In time I'll be able to proclaim my love for you to the world." He seals his promise with another kiss, which quickens Athena's pulse.

Athena is calmer after talking to Jon, who puts her fears at rest, and just being with him is comforting. She looks forward to his kisses and his touch. My loving Englishman, she calls him. Her word for him in Spanish is *cariñoso*, which she picked up from her father, whose own father was part Spanish. The lineage explains their Spanish surname "Bravo", which means "brave", and also used to mean "fine" and "excellent" in praise of a performance.

Chapter 19

Advocacy

On the first few months of his retirement, Rodrigo finds himself with plenty of time on his hands. He is used to always having something to do. He rarely missed a day of work when he was still employed. He toys with the idea of doing volunteer work for a worthy cause within San Francisco. He discusses this with Marina, and they agree to search for an advocacy which focuses on the poor. Rodrigo spends time in cyberspace looking for the right group to join.

In his searches, he discovers that the main concern of the poor, aside from food, is housing. He fails to understand why there are many homeless families in a rich country like America, including San Francisco. He plunges into a comprehensive study on this, asks questions, and talks to people to expand his knowledge of the present situation.

He learns that several groups have staged strikes at the City Hall questioning the Quality Housing Responsibility Act passed in 1998 by the San Francisco Housing

Authority because it disqualifies undocumented families from Section 8 housing and the public housing, which are in turn awarded to the middle class. This is because it reserves 60% of the housing units for families with between 30% and 80% of the median income. It puts the poor at a disadvantage since 70% of San Francisco residents fall below 30%, so that will leave them without homes.

The groups point out that the city has signed into the Declaration of Human Rights, which recognizes housing as a human right. In view of this, San Francisco should also embrace refugees and immigrants. The striking groups demand a fair treatment by eliminating the required documentation of families, according equal rights to everyone in the waiting list, and providing a fund for displaced families.

Rodrigo cannot imagine what can be worse than living in the streets without shelter, and his heart goes out to those families that will be directly affected, and most of these families include children. He finally decides to register with the Coalition on Homelessness to offer his support and service to the group. It is a social justice organization, which promotes advocacy for the homeless to reach long-term solutions of poverty, homelessness, and housing in San Francisco.

Coalition on Homelessness was founded in 1987, and is composed of service providers, homeless people, and activists. Rodrigo thinks he will probably fall under the "activists" category since he is fighting for a cause. His regard for advocacy groups is raised a notch higher as he considers the personal efforts they put in to effect change and support a cause, and these are usually *pro bono*. He visits their office and quickly registers.

Jon has not yet divulged to Athena his weekend advocacy. For the past year, he has been offering free legal service to the poor and the homeless. It is his way of sharing his talents and blessings with them. At Coalition on Homelessness, he manages the Shelter Grievance Policy, which allows residents to have legal course when they get evicted from their shelters. His services include filing a lawsuit if the issue is a matter of civil law, mediation and arbitration before a dispute goes to court, petition to a legislature for a change in the law if it appears to be unjust, and of course, free legal advice. Jon shares this with Athena.

"Shall we say, it's my weekend service, or Saturday escape, if you can call it that," he tells her after explaining to her his chosen advocacy.

"How wonderful, Jon. You're such a kind person to be doing something for others for free. I'm impressed. Can I join you one Saturday? I'd love to see you at work."

"I'd be more than happy to have you with me. At least we can be together. How about this coming Saturday?"

"Okay. Oh, I'm so excited. Do you actually go to court to defend a case?"

"Sometimes, but I assist more in the mediation and arbitration, and also in the preparation if there's a court case involved. There are other young volunteer lawyers. I guide them. It's also good training for them."

"You never cease to amaze me, Jon," Athena expresses her admiration.

"Thank you for believing in me, love," he responds, utterly pleased. "I'll pick you up Saturday morning, nine-ish? Come in jeans or something casual."

"I'll be ready."

CHAPTER 20

Chance Encounter

Athena waits for Jon and is gung ho in anticipation of the day's event. He arrives at her building lobby promptly at 9:00 a.m. He is in a white casual Marks & Spencer shirt, jeans, and sneakers, and Athena admires his casual look. She wears a light blue blouse, jeans, and matching *espadrilles*. Jon gives her the look-over and comments.

"Good morning, my pretty girlfriend. You look fresh and lovely," which makes Athena blush slightly.

"Good morning to you, Jon. You look good yourself."

They give each other a quick kiss, and she detects the pleasant aroma of his after-shave lotion. They proceed to the office of Coalition on Homelessness, and the office is already abuzz with activity. Everyone there knows Jon and welcomes him warmly.

"This is my girlfriend, Athena Bravo," Jon introduces her. Athena greets everyone present.

"Bravo? The name sounds familiar," says one of the staff, knitting his brow as if trying hard to remember something. Rodrigo had just registered a week ago.

Jon leads Athena to a medium-size room where there are already people sitting or milling around. They all greet Jon with a ready smile. More introductions. The five people in the group drag their chairs to form a circle. Jon insists that Athena sit next to him. He begins by telling the group that they are pursuing their grievance on the Quality Housing Responsibility Act. They need to prepare a petition to a legislature to show that it is unjust towards the poor. Jon assigns a young lawyer to draft the petition. There is a case of a resident evicted from his shelter. Jon reviews the case and says that the resident has a right to fight it out in court. There are more issues on the agenda, and Jon deals with them in a professional manner. Athena listens attentively. She is full of admiration for her boyfriend, and can see what a great lawyer he is.

After an hour passes, they take a coffee break. Athena suddenly has an "aha" moment, and asks Jon.

"Do they have a newsletter? Maybe I can volunteer to write or edit for them."

"Of course, they do. It's called '*Street Sheet*'. I can talk to the person in-charge about it. Wait here." Jon leaves the room briefly.

Rodrigo passes by and does a double-take when he notices Athena. He enters the room and approaches her.

"Athena, what are you doing here?" She is as surprised as he is.

"Dad, why are you here?" They hug.

"I registered for volunteer work only last week since I'm not that busy anymore. How about you?," he asks her. Just then, Jon returns to the room and approaches them.

"Dad, this is Jonathan Prentiss, a partner at Blake, Johnson, and Prentiss Law Office. He volunteered his legal service here. Jon is my boyfriend."

Rodrigo's eyes widen at the revelation. He smiles and shakes Jon's extended hand.

"Nice to meet you, Mr. Bravo," Jon responds. "Athena wants to see me at work. I talked to the person in-charge if she can volunteer for the newsletter, and he says she's more than welcome here," Jon reports, shifting his gaze to Athena. "You're in. '*Street Sheet*' has the largest circulation of street newspapers with 32,000 monthly copies distributed."

"That's great, so we're all in this together," Rodrigo replies. "What a coincidence that we volunteered for the same cause. How long have you been doing this, Jon, may I ask?"

"For a year now, sir. I find it very fulfilling."

"It must be. I'm just new here and I'm feeling that already. It's a good idea for you to be involved too, Athena."

"I know that, Dad."

"Well, I have to be in the next room. It was good meeting you, Jon. Take care of my baby."

"I will, Mr. Bravo. You can be sure of that," he answers, and Rodrigo believes him.

Athena accompanies her dad to the door and whispers to him.

"Dad, please don't tell Mom yet about Jon and me. I don't want Diana to know. I had a bad experience with her with my past boyfriend."

"I understand, Athena. It's our little secret. Jon seems such a fine and smart young man, and handsome too." He winks at her. "He sounds English."

"He was born in England, but has lived here for many years. He's half English and half American."

"I like him. Do you love him?"

"I do, Dad, and he loves me too."

"That's all that matters, Athena."

Athena tells Jon that her dad is impressed with him, and he is glad to hear that. They continue to review other cases on the agenda. When they are finished at almost noon, Jon says:

"I feel like a burger. What do you say to that?"

"I'd like one too. McDonald's?"

McDonald's it is, and coffee afterwards at Starbucks. They share a preference for coffee.

CHAPTER 21

A Wedding

At work, Athena's phone rings, and it is Barbara.

"Athena, let's have lunch. I've something very important to tell you. Can we meet downstairs at noon?"

"Sure, Barbs. Sounds urgent. See you later."

"I'm getting married!" Barbara announces with excitement as they take their seats at the restaurant.

"I'm happy for you, Barbs. When is the big event?"

"Next month. It will just be a small wedding because Angelo and I are saving for our future. He still has to finish his medical studies. Athena, will you be my maid of honor?"

"Of course, Barbs. I'm honored that you chose me."

"I want to meet your boyfriend, and I'm also inviting him to the wedding. I've heard good things about him, you know."

"I'll tell Jon. I'm sure he'd want to meet you and Angelo too."

When Athena tells Jon, he suggests inviting them to dinner. He wants to meet Athena's friends. They dine in a Chinese restaurant and pick a booth for more private conversations. They talk animatedly about their respective jobs and Angelo's medical studies, including their volunteer work. Barbara is a talker and fits in well in advertising. Jon believes she is a loyal friend to Athena, and he likes her. Angelo is the serious type and focused on becoming a doctor. Later in the powder room, Barbara admits to Athena:

"I like Jon very much, so brilliant and good-looking. Has your twin met him?"

"Not yet," Athena replies.

"Oh, oh. I hope it's not going to be a *déjà vu*."

"What do you mean?"

"Look back to what happened in the past, Athena. Just be careful. He's a good catch, and your twin might steal him from you," Barbara warns her.

"Not this time," Athena promises.

"Go, girl," Barbara encourages her.

Barbara and Angelo's wedding is small and cozy, held in the community chapel with the reception at the courtyard. Their color motif is peach, and Athena's gown is of the same color, which compliments her complexion. Jon appreciates how she looks.

"You're glowing. I can imagine how you'll look in your own wedding," he hints, and her face reddens with his comment.

The guest list is a mixture of cultures - Barbara's Chinese relatives, Angelo's Hispanic progeny, and their close American friends. The couple's respective families are already US-born and consider themselves Americans. After the ceremonial cutting of the cake, Barbara asks the women to gather for the throwing of the bouquet. First, she looks back to see where Athena is standing before she hurls her bouquet, which lands at Athena's feet. Athena picks it up embarrassed. She takes a peek at Jon, and he is grinning at her and applauding.

"You didn't seem eager to catch the bouquet." Jon comments afterwards.

"I'm never eager for such things," Athena replies. "It was intentional on Barbara's part. I'm sure she wanted me to catch it. She must have planned it all along."

Athena welcomes the dancing because she likes being in Jon's arms, and he happens to be an excellent dancer. How she wishes it would go on forever.

CHAPTER 22

Reversal of Character

Just two months after her sojourn in Paris, Diana is already showing signs of the return of her old character. Although she and Pierre still communicate through e-mail, she yearns for the physical contact. Her feeling of restlessness prods her to revert to her promiscuous self. It is ironic that she earlier feared Pierre would get attracted to other women in her absence, but now she is living her own fear by fooling around. Pierre does not know about it, being miles away, and he is now an out-of-sight-out-of-mind commodity.

In spite of her wantonness, Diana does not just go after any man, but she picks the handsome and *macho* ones. Her taste for a particular type of men is known to her friends, and she is adept at seducing them simply with her good looks and sexy body. What sets her apart from hookers is that she is not into it for the money or anything else of material value, but for the sheer pleasure and conquest.

Diana has her own rules with regard to her conquests. For one, she keeps her distance from married men to avoid complications with their wives. Upon her return to San Francisco, the old Diana surfaces. Her first conquest is Kevin, the nicely sculpted gym instructor in the gym she registers in. He has an Adonis physique with a boyish charm. When their eyes meet on her first day there, it is obvious that the attraction is mutual. At the end of the day, the relationship is sealed. She stays in the gym until closing time, and they have the place to themselves. It begins in the shower room, all the way to the mats and benches. She finds Kevin not only an experienced lover, but also an imaginative one.

She visits the gym almost everyday, and Kevin personally supervises her use of the machines which gives him a chance to seemingly unconsciously touch her to Diana's satisfaction. This goes on for a few months. Diana is the type who loves to relate her sexual adventures to her gang, and they are her avid listeners. They know about Pierre too. Their gatherings are usually enlivened with Diana's interesting stories and juicy accounts. Her friends are in awe of her experiences with men.

Diana is not a one-man woman, except when she was with Pierre in Paris, and Kevin is not her only conquest. She soon tires of him when she realizes that they cannot communicate intelligently, and their common interest is limited to sex. Kevin is not a smart kind of guy. His world revolves around physical fitness, and he has the right muscles to prove that. He eventually bores Diana, and she tells him it is over between them. Diana is a smart woman, and she enjoys intellectual tussles with men. Kevin is not up to par with her in this area.

She even goes for a one-night stand if she finds the guy attractive, then decides afterwards if he is interesting enough. After Kevin, she has other conquests, but her succeeding relationships are no more than a week or two. Usually she is the one who initiates the break-up.

Then she meets Paolo, who is a chef in his own popular Italian restaurants, and in his 30s. She is having dinner with three of her close friends at *Paolo's* when Chef Paolo Romano walks in and talks to the patrons. Diana is mesmerized when she catches sight of him as she ogles this jaw-dropping and tall Italian with dark features, tousled black hair, and piercing eyes. When he stops at their table, she openly flirts with him and is all praises for his cooking. Paolo is likewise captivated by her, and is receptive to her charm. Diana's friends observe that he pays particular attention to her, and he barely notices them.

"It's an honor to meet the chef and owner of this fine restaurant," Diana compliments Paolo.

"*Gracie, signorina,*" he reacts.

"I notice you're not wearing you chef's hat," Diana comments.

"Oh, you mean that tall hat? I wear that only when I'm cooking," he explains in his Italian accent.

"I'm Diana and I'm interested in culinary arts. May I seek your advice some time?," she asks him.

"Of course, Diana," he responds. "Here's my calling card. Call me anytime you're ready."

He then kisses her hand as he looks into her eyes, and says "*Arrivederci*", then takes his leave. She is hooked. For a moment, the hand-kissing brings back memories of European chivalry. Her friends are all excited.

"Diana, he likes you," says one of her friends enthusiastically.

"I heard he's married, so he's out of your league," counters another friend. "He has the reputation of having been around women too."

"I like him. Hmm. He's verile-looking and very masculine. I may have to break my rule on the 'married' thing. He's Italian, and they're very passionate lovers," Diana expresses her opinion. Her friends all stare at her. "I should have learned Italian, but never mind, maybe he can teach me," she enunciates with confidence, implying that she has the capacity to tempt him.

Chapter 23

Dangerous Liaison

Diana does not waste time in getting to Paolo. She knows she has a way with men. When she calls him and says she wants to see him, he does not hesitate to suggest his office at the restaurant. Diana goes there in a mini skirt and a blouse with a décolletage, and his admiration is evident. She immediately senses his interest in her by the way he gives her a look replete with passion. The mutual attraction is so potent that they are drawn to each other like magnets, and they move towards each other simultaneously. Before they know it, they are kissing and fondling with unbridled desire in the privacy of his office. They pull away only when there is a knock on the door, and Paolo opens it to answer a question from his staff. Then they resume what they are doing uninterrupted for a long period of time.

"I want to see you again," he tells her huskily, and she quickly agrees.

"Meet me at the Grand Hotel tonight. I have a regular room there, Room 802. Here's the key. I'll leave the restaurant early. Be there at 7:00. We can have room service. Can you stay for the night?," he asks her with hope in his voice.

"Yes, I want to if that's all right with you," she replies.

"More than all right. See you tonight, okay?" He gives her a long hard kiss before they part.

The affair with Paolo remains strong because Diana is satisfied with his sexual prowess, and Paolo has a wit of his own. They can discuss all sorts of topics because he is a man of the world and is well-traveled. They just have to be extra careful because he is married, and he wants to keep her away from his wife. He is totally smitten with Diana.

"You're very beautiful, Diana. I can't get enough of you," he confesses in his Italian accent, which awakens her desire. *Why do I get aroused with foreign accent?*

Their lovemaking is intense, and Paolo is an emotional lover, even better than Pierre. During their intimate moments, he shouts her name and utters *la mia stella* (my star) or *mio amore* (my darling) to her. This does wonders to Diana's self-image. She becomes an obsequious partner when her lover puts her on a pedestal. Now with Paolo, she wants to please him and make him happy because he is the perfect lover to her.

"Paolo, I have a confession to make," she starts to tell him, while they lie in bed. He props his head on his elbow and looks down at her with raised eyebrows.

"What I told you when we first met about my interest in the culinary arts was just a pretext. I really wanted to get to you," she continues.

"I'm glad, otherwise I wouldn't have known you like this. Oh, Diana, Diana, *sto cadendo nell'amore con voi.* " he tells her passionately.

"Please translate that. I like how it sounds. You should teach me Italian."

"I said that I'm falling in love with you, Diana. You're my goddess."

"I can't explain my feelings for you too. It's just that you're not free."

"I can leave my wife for you, but you have to give me time. She can create a problem if she finds out about you, that's why we have to be careful. She doesn't know about this hotel room, so we're safe here. *Capisce?* (Understand).

Diana has to be content with meeting Paolo on the sly. The ultimate chance for them to be together for the entire time comes when Diana goes on her annual leave, and Paolo suggests they travel to Italy together. It is definitely her happiest moment ever being with Paolo every minute of the day and exploring the Italian countryside with him.

They visit Tuscany, and she gets to meet his parents and big family. They seem to be simple folks, friendly and hospitable. She loves listening to Paolo speak in his native Italian with the people there and gesture with his hands as Italians do. He introduces her to the delicacies of the provinces they visit. What tickles her most is when they address her as *Signora Romano* (Mrs. Romano), and not *Signorina* (Miss). The people there regard them as honeymooners who are madly in love with each other by the way they behave. Just when Diana wishes she were married to someone like Paolo, it is not possible.

This is one facet of her romantic escapades she does not share with her friends because she wants to guard Paolo's reputation. She also does not want to get him into trouble with his wife. What matters to her now are his well-being and happiness. She asks herself if this is love this time. She is overwhelmed with her feelings for Paolo, more than with Pierre. Her world now revolves around Paolo, and just looking at him makes her pulsate with indescribable emotion. She realizes that the bitterness comes from its being a forbidden love.

Chapter 24

Familiarity

Loving a person entails knowing that person well and becoming familiar with the good and the not-so-good traits. Lovers bare their idiosyncrasies, weaknesses, strengths, and even secrets to each other, otherwise the lack or absence of transparency can erode the relationship. A relationship rooted in complete honesty has the greatest chance of survival.

From the start, Diana and Paolo have been honest towards each other. Paolo did not keep his marital status from her, and he admitted that he had many affairs in the past. Diana also revealed to him her former indiscretions. They are both living in the "now" and are happy just being together.

"What's your wife like?," she asks him from out of the blue.

"She's not anything like you. She's Italian with a fiery temper. She's not concerned about me, but only that I provide for her and our son. The problem is, we married hastily. Don't worry about it for now, *amore* (beloved). I'm going to do something about it."

⎯⎯ ⋯⊷⊶⊷⊷⊶⊷⋯ ⎯⎯

Paolo immediately seeks the advice of a lawyer friend of his about the possibility of divorce. Where he comes from, the prenuptial agreement is not a common document, so when he and his wife got married in Italy, there was no such thing. His friend tells him that the divorce may cost him half of what he is worth because it is conjugal. Paolo owns two restaurants, which are doing very well. Apart from that, he has investments, and he owns an apartment in Manhattan and a house in Tuscany, aside from the condo in San Francisco, so he is a wealthy man. His friend explains that a really good lawyer knows the nuances of the law and will find the best settlement deal for his client.

⎯⎯ ⋯⊷⊶⊷⊷⊶⊷⋯ ⎯⎯

As their steady relationship progresses, Jon and Athena are aware that they still have a lot to know about each other, but so far they are happy with how their relationship is developing, and every day they uncover new facets of each other's characters. Athena finds it exciting discovering Jon's likes and dislikes. They are both wide readers, so a visit to the library is something they both relish, even if they can order books on Amazon. "It's the experience of being surrounded by books that's different," Jon articulates.

They also share a preference for health foods. The exceptions to that are ice cream and chocolates, which they occasionally indulge in. Aside from the library, a visit to the gym is a three-times-a-week "must" since they intend to keep fit. Athena enroled in the gym Jon frequents. Jon likes watching action and crime movies, while she is more into romance and real-life stories. As a compromise, they give way to each other's choices. When they do not go to the cinema, they watch films either at Jon's or Athena's condo, as an indoor date complete with popcorn.

Jon introduces her to the art of dancing. She gets to like dancing with Jon's lead. He teaches her how to swing, fox trot, boogie, and waltz at his more spacious place. She likes being in Jon's arms, and guided by him. At times, they go to a place where there is dancing, and she is able to practice her newly learned steps with Jon. Their music preferences are more eclectic, and they often just sit and listen to his collection.

Swimming is one sport they both indulge in at their condos' pools or at Jon's Club. Athena watches actual NBA, baseball, and soccer games plus tennis matches with Jon or on television since she is a sports fan like him. The only thing they do not agree on is spicy food. Jon likes spicy food, which Athena does not go for. They enrich their own spheres of interest by adopting or learning something from each other.

"Thanks for teaching me how to dance. I love it," Athena tells Jon. "I should reciprocate and teach you something I know too. How about sign language? I'm good at it since I volunteered in High School to teach the deaf."

"Really? Do you think I'll have some use for it?"

"Why not? Suppose you'll need to defend a deaf client, it might just come in handy. I know that often there are interpreters in the court room for such cases, but it would be an advantage if you know what is being said."

"Okay, I'm interested to learn. Besides, I think I like my teacher," he admits jokingly.

Athena holds on to her no-sex rule. Jon understands and respects it. She explains to him nicely that she wants to save herself for the man she will marry. He loves her all the more for being a principled woman. He is content with kissing and hugging her, with the certainty that they will eventually marry.

"I'll honor that. I'm confident I'm the man you'll marry," he states. "Besides, intimacy is not always about sex."

CHAPTER 25

Legalities

When Paolo asks his lawyer friend to suggest the best lawyer, one name crops up: Jonathan Prentiss. Paolo has not heard of him, and asks his friend for more details.

"If you really want the best, that's Jonathan Prentiss of the Blake, Johnson, and Prentiss Law Office," the friend recommends. "He wins his cases, and he has a fine track record of handling divorces. He's damn good."

"No need to curse. I'll take your word for it. I'll call him and ask for an appointment. He must be expensive coming from a prestigious firm. Anyway, money is no obstacle."

Paolo called up the law firm the following day and talks to Jon's secretary, who tells him that Jon's calendar is full, and he can be accommodated next week. Paolo is willing to wait. When the appointment date finally comes, Paolo is ushered into Jon's office by his secretary Amanda.

"Hello, Mr. Romano. Aren't you that famous chef of *Paolo's*? I recognize you," Jon greets him. They shake hands.

"Yes, that's me, Mr. Prentiss."

"You serve good food. My girlfriend and I have eaten there."

"Thank you for patronizing my restaurant."

"Have a seat. What can I do for you?" Paolo settles down on the armchair and Jon sits on the other armchair facing it.

"I want to divorce my wife, and I need your help."

"Okay. Do you have any particular reason for resorting to divorce?"

"We've not been getting along for a long time. We married in haste. I met somebody whom I'm in love with. My problem is I have assets I don't want my wife to get her hands on. We also have a son I don't want to lose."

"How old is your son?"

"Luigi is five years old now. What do you want me to do, Mr. Prentiss? I'll pay any amount for your service."

"First, Mr. Romano, I want you to list down your assets and their corresponding values. On your next visit, we'll discuss each one of them."

"The thing is, Mr. Prentiss, we didn't sign a prenuptial agreement. Does that mean that half of what I own will go to my wife?"

"Not necessarily. We'll see what we can do. That's why I need to discuss with you every detail of your assets. There are legal solutions available, and we try to find the best one for our client."

"I have another concern, Mr. Prentiss. Right now my wife doesn't know about my girlfriend Diana. What if she finds out about my affair and files a case of concubinage ahead of the divorce, does it change anything?" Jon is slightly astonished at the mention of his girlfriend's name.

"It will still be about your assets and the custody of your son. Our role is to see to it that you will retain most of your assets and share custody of your son."

"That's a relief to hear. I will provide you with a list of my assets on my next visit. As much as possible, I don't want my girlfriend involved."

"All right then, Mr. Romano. By the way, what is the name of your girlfriend again?"

"Diana Bravo."

———

Jon heard the name right. *Diana Bravo, Athena's twin, is Chef Paolo's mistress, and he wants to divorce his wife.* He shares the information with Athena, who is stunned with the revelation.

Chapter 26

Questions

"How did that happen, Jon? Diana, the mistress of Chef Paolo? I never would have guessed," Athena is dismayed upon hearing Jon's report.

"He seems seriously in love with her, and he wants to divorce his wife."

"I've known all along that Diana has had numerous relationships, but I think only with unattached males. Why Chef Paolo? He's married."

"There are things we can't explain when it comes to love, Athena. She must be in love with him too. He's a very attractive self-made man. Even Amanda, my secretary, has a crush on him."

"Really? Now you pique my curiosity, Jon. I want to go to his restaurant to catch a glimpse of him and see for myself." Jon finds her suggestion amusing.

"Okay, love, I'll take you to dinner there," he tells her with a smile. "I know he usually comes out and talks to the diners, but we didn't see him when we were there. I've seen him once before I met you when I had dinner with friends at *Paolo's*."

—⁓•☙❦☙•⁓—

On the next weekend, Jon takes Athena to *Paolo's* for dinner. He acquiesces to Athena's enthusiasm. She orders *ravioli*, while Jon has the *pasta putanesca*. They are enjoying their meal with white wine when Paolo comes out and greets the diners. He spots Jon and approaches their table. Jon stands to shake his hand.

"Mr. Prentiss, I'm glad to see you here."

"We like the food here, Mr. Romano. This is my girlfriend, Athena."

"How do you do," he says to Athena. "*Bellisima*" (very beautiful), taking her hand and kissing it. His greeting indicates that he is taken by Athena's beauty.

"Pleased to meet you, Chef Paolo," she responds, appreciating his hand-kissing gesture.

"Is your girlfriend here?," Jon asks him, and Athena throws Jon a warning look.

"No. We avoid being seen together," he whispers to Jon.

"I understand," Jon answers.

"Enjoy your meal. I'll see you soon," patting Jon's shoulder. "Nice meeting you," he tells Athena, bowing slightly, then takes his leave.

"I hope he doesn't mention my name to Diana. How many Athenas are there? She might suspect."

"Well?," Jon asks.

"Well, what?"

"What do you think of him? That's what we came here for, remember?"

"Oh, right. He's very attractive and chivalrous. You can't blame Diana for falling for his looks and charm. She has a weakness for handsome guys. However, let me tell you this, Jon. He pales in comparison with you."

"You're very funny, Athena, but thanks for the compliment."

"I mean it. In my opinion, you're much more good-looking than he is. You're my knight in shining armor, Jon." He is evidently pleased.

"Watch it. If you keep flattering me like that, I may not be able to keep myself from kissing you roughly right here, and I won't stop even if you beg." Athena is aroused by what he threatens to do.

"Would you really do that?," she whispers.

"I would too, and it will be my pleasure." Athena blushes, and Jon is smiling at her discomfiture.

CHAPTER 27

Settlement

On Paolo's succeeding visit to Jon's office, they go through his list of assets and put down the corresponding value of each. Jon learns that he is worth millions. Jon reveals to him that he need not concede half of it to his wife when he files for divorce.

"That's wonderful news, Mr. Prentiss."

"Hey, call me Jon. It's okay to be on first-name basis."

"Does my wife have any right to demand more, Jon?"

"We'll make her an offer she cannot refuse, with your approval of course, Paolo. How about your girlfriend? Is she not interested in your money perhaps?"

"No, no. Diana is not the least bit concerned about how much I'm worth, and she doesn't even know nor does she bother to ask. She has a good job and has money of her own. I love her, Jon, and I've never felt loved like this before. This is the woman for me, and I plan to make her my wife when the divorce is final."

"Good, then we only have your wife to worry about. Before we file the divorce case, let's ready our offer to her, so we're prepared. How often do you want to see your son Luigi? Is every weekend and on certain holidays okay with you?"

"I'd be happy with that schedule. I have to understand that he needs to go to school too, and the condo is closer to his school. I love that boy, Jon, and any time spent with him is precious to me."

———

After further discussions with Paolo, Jon shows him the settlement offer he suggests they present to his wife. Jon believes that if he gives her the condo in San Francisco where they presently reside in, she may not take interest in his other real estate property. This is the breakdown of Paolo's offer:

San Francisco condo
$2 million in cash
Luigi's education and personal needs
Joint child custody

Luigi will live with his mother and spend Christmas and certain holidays with her, including half of his school summer holidays. The boy will be with Paolo from 6:00 p.m. Friday until 6:00 p.m. Sunday, and also on Thanksgiving, Easter, and New Year. He will also spend half of his school summer holidays with his father. Paolo is satisfied with the arrangement of shared time with his son, whom he loves dearly.

Jon agrees to meet once more with Paolo to deal with the nitty-gritty of the case before they formally file the divorce papers. Jon is in for a jolt as Paolo saunters into his office with Diana in tow. He suddenly remembers

Athena's framed photo on his desk, so he leads them to the receiving area in his office.

"Jon, this is my girlfriend Diana," he introduces her with seeming pride.

"How do you do, Diana. Paolo speaks highly of you."

"Does he?," she pokes Paolo lightly in the ribs. She eyes Jon with admiration, which confirms her instant appreciation of his totality.

"Of course, *amore*. I wanted Jon to meet you so he can see why I've fallen in love with you."

"The feeling is mutual, Paolo," she responds. She turns to Jon. "So, you're English. Paolo tells me how good a lawyer you are."

"Well, thank you. We always try to do our best for our clients." He looks at Paolo.

"I can foresee a victory for you here, Paolo. Let me present our offer to your wife enticingly. As a last resort, we can hint that if she doesn't sign, we are willing to go to court. That usually makes the other party think it over carefully since a court case can be a lengthy business."

After leaving Jon's office, Diana gives her opinion of him to Paolo.

"Your lawyer is quite impressive and experienced. He really knows what to do. You picked the right one." She does not admit to him that her own description of Jon on the outside is in the superlative, and she finds him extraordinarily smart and gorgeous.

"Guess who I met today. You won't believe it," Jon greets Athena.

"Let me guess. Is it a celebrity? George Clooney perhaps?" He shakes his head. "Oh, c'mon tell me, Jon," she pleads. He takes her into his arms, and she becomes suspicious.

"Not Diana?," she ventures a guess. He looks down at her with a hint of a smile on his face.

"It's Diana!, she exclaims, looking up at him, and he nods.

"Well, how did it happen? How was she?"

"She was okay. Paolo wanted me to meet her. He's undoubtedly in love with her. It appears she's not interested in his money. She's beautiful, Athena, but not as beautiful as you. You know, you don't look alike, and there's very little resemblance. Are you sure you're twins?"

———∿∿◦○❦◐❧○◦∿∿———

Paolo does not tarry, and he files for divorce through Jon's law firm. His wife Natalia does not offer any resistance and agrees to meet with Paolo and Jon at the Blake, Johnson, and Prentiss Law Office for a negotiation discussion. She is accompanied by her own lawyer. Natalia is a dark beauty, and her appearance suggests a fighting spirit behind her façade. Jon judges her as adversarial by her demeanor, and not the sweet type. She is civil towards Paolo.

Jon does the talking and presents their offer with embellishments of his own. In his articulate and brilliant way, he stresses that she need not worry about living accommodations because Paolo is giving her their condo, plus a generous monetary settlement of $2 million to see to it that she is well provided for. The amount will free her of money problems. He assures her that she will have main custody of their son, who will be with her most of the time, and will be with Paolo on weekends. Paolo will also pay for Luigi's education and personal expenses, so she will have no worries when it comes to their son's welfare and needs.

Jon weaves an attractive package, which gives the offer a more-than- generous character. Natalia's eyes widen as she listens to Jon. She scans through the offer details on paper, then consults her lawyer in whispers. In a matter of minutes, she agrees and signs the divorce papers, to Paolo's relief. Paolo is completely satisfied and gives Jon a bear hug in gratitude.

CHAPTER 28

Attraction

Diana cannot dismiss the image of Jonathan Prentiss from her mind. She admits to herself that he is very good-looking and exudes magnetism by the way he talks and moves. Those penetrating blue eyes haunt her. She finds herself intrigued by this man, who happens to be also a brilliant lawyer. What bothers her is that he did not seem taken by her when they met, the way most men are, which is something she is used to. There was not the slightest indication that he found her attractive, and he spoke to her perfunctorily in a business-like manner. She cannot accept that.

She can usually tell from the expression in a man's face when her beauty attracts him. There was none of that from Jon. This is a blow to her ego. Diana thinks that he may be gay, and she decides that it is imperative that she knows for sure about his sexuality without Paolo's knowledge. So she plots her move to have a legitimate excuse of seeing Jon and judge him for herself.

—⁓⦿⧲⦿⧲⦿⧲⦿⁓—

"JP, Diana Bravo is here and would like to see you," Amanda advises him as she enters his office. "She has no appointment."

"You mean she's alone? Did she say what her purpose is?"

"She says she has to consult you about something legal."

"I can squeeze her in only for a few minutes since I need to be at my 2:00 p.m. meeting, so please don't forget to remind me later. Okay, send her in." Jon hurriedly takes Athena's framed photo on his desk and keeps it inside the drawer.

Diana enters his office wearing a short tight-fitting red dress and in high heels. They greet each other, and Jon offers her a chair, while he sits across her. As she sits down, her skirt goes up her thighs when she crosses her legs provocatively, and Jon catches a glimpse of her underwear, but he pretends not to notice.

"I understand you want to consult me about a legal matter. Does Paolo know about this?"

"I don't want Paolo to know about this. It's no legal matter really."

"Oh, what is it then?"

She pauses, then crosses and uncrosses her legs seductively on purpose, revealing her red underwear, which matches the color of her dress, and Jon continues to remain oblivious of what she is doing.

"I just want your opinion about something. I'm confused about the idea of marrying Paolo, whether it's the right decision. I want to know what you think of him," she proceeds.

"You're the best judge of that, Diana. You're closer to him, and you've known him longer."

"You must have your impression of him. You see, I don't know who else to ask."

"Why are you asking me of all people? I was just his lawyer and nothing more. I'm really not the best person to ask."

"You had dealings with him, so I thought you'd be able to tell me. Women in general are drawn to him, but I want a male perspective, and you're the only one I can approach, Jon."

"This is most unusual, Diana. I've nothing to tell you, except perhaps that Paolo seems such a great guy. If you truly love him, you should marry him. That doesn't sound like a legal advice, does it? Maybe you should just follow your heart." She does not appear satisfied with Jon's response. She pauses for a half minute.

"May I ask you a personal question, Jon?

"Yes, go ahead."

"Are you gay?" Jon's face registers astonishment, but he manages to smile since he finds Diana's question funny.

"No, I'm not gay, Diana," he stresses. "If you want to know if I'm attracted to Paolo, the answer is no. I'm heterosexual and I have a girlfriend whom I love very much." *If you only know who she is.* Then Amanda interrupts him with a reminder: "JP, you have a meeting. It's almost 2:00."

"I'm sorry if I have to cut this short. I hope I've answered your questions," he addresses Diana. He then accompanies her to the door and bids her goodbye. She realizes that her seduction tactics have no effect on Jon, and this is her first let-down. She concludes, *He must really be in love with his girlfriend, whoever she is.*

—◦◦◦—

"She tried to seduce you?," Athena expresses disbelief.

"If you can consider showing one's underwear as a form of seduction," Jon replies.

"Of course, it is. I can't believe it. Barbara was right, and she warned me about this. It's Philip all over again, but this time she's not out to spite me because she doesn't know that you're my boyfriend. Diana is not monogamous then because she already has Paolo, but she still attempted to tempt you. You must have caught her fancy, Jon. She likes handsome and intelligent men."

"Are you flattering me again, huh?," he jokes.

"Seriously, Jon, she must find you attractive for her to do that."

"In fact, I didn't give her the slightest interest. She probably thought I was gay because I didn't show any attraction towards her."

"What if she finds out you're my boyfriend?"

"That would be the day. She's bound to find out sooner or later, anyway."

"Thank you for not surrendering to Diana's advances."

"That's highly impossible, darling, because I love you, and I will never do something that will hurt you."

CHAPTER 29

A Court Case

Athena's wish to witness Jon's performance in court finally comes true. She and Barbara take the morning off from work to be present in court. Jon defends a man who is accused of shooting another man and is implicated by a witness. Jon looks dashing in his navy blue suit with a striped tie, and Athena admires him from a distance. He spots them and waves before the start of the proceedings. The case takes approximately two hours. This is the tail-end of Jon's cross-examination of the witness:

Jon: "Mr. Stein, you testified that you witnessed the actual shooting."

Witness: "Yes, that's right."

Jon: "How far away were you from where the actual shooting occurred?"

Witness: "About 25 feet away."

Jon: "Where were you at the very moment when the gun was fired?"

Witness: "I was hiding behind a tombstone."

Jon: "What were you doing there at 11 o'clock in the evening?"

Witness: "I was just passing through when I heard the commotion. I hid and peeked."

Jon: "Mr. Stein, you said that you saw the defendant actually shoot the victim?"

Witness: 'Yes, that's correct.'

Jon: "Can you describe the incident which you said you witnessed?"

Witness: "I heard two men arguing and shouting. Then this guy took out his gun and shot the other guy."

Jon: "Did you actually see the shooter's face?"

Witness: "Yes, I did."

Jon: "Is that person inside the courtroom?"

Witness: "Yes."

Jon: "Please point him out to the court." (The witness points at the defendant)

Jon: "Are you absolutely certain?"

Witness: "Yes."

Jon: "Is this the gun used in the shooting?" (Jon produces the gun as evidence and shows it to the witness).

Witness: "Yes, it looks like the same one."

Jon: "You don't seem sure about that."

Witness: "Yes, I'm more or less sure."

Jon: "Could you see very well that night?"

Witness: "Yes."

Jon: "Were there lights in the cemetery when this happened?"

Witness: "Yes."

Jon: "What was your source of light during the night of the shooting?"

Witness: "There's a lamppost at the curb, so I could see everything clearly."

Jon: "Let me summarize your answers, Mr. Stein. You saw the actual shooting. You recognized the defendant. You recognized the gun. All of these at a distance of 25 feet, and your only source of light was from the lamppost. Am I right?"

Witness: "Yes, that's what I said."

Jon then produces a document from the electric company and presents it to the court as evidence, then he addresses the court.

Jon: "Your honor, this document which I present as evidence offers proof that there was no light coming from that particular lamppost on the night of the shooting. The electric company's report says that there was a circuitry problem with this particular post late that afternoon which was fixed only the next day. It is obvious from the cross-examination that there are flaws in this witness' testimony. The evidence establishes that there was indeed no light from the lamppost on the night of the shooting, contrary to what the witness told the court, so it was impossible for him to have seen anything, especially at a distance of 25 feet."

"Furthermore, my client could not have been the perpetrator of the crime. From earlier testimonies, we learned that my client was not even anywhere near the scene of the crime when it was committed. We have proven that he was at home with his family from 8:00 p.m. until the next morning. Therefore, I request the court to dismiss the case against my client."

Athena and Barbara are impressed with Jon's defence. He has a dynamic presence in court and, without doubt, a perspicacious lawyer. The court cleared his client of the crime.

"You were brilliant, Jon," Barbara comments when they meet outside the courtroom after the trial.

"My hero," Athena says as she hugs him.

"Thanks to my two loyal fans. For that, I'm inviting you to lunch."

CHAPTER 30

Changes

Paolo has replaced Pierre in Diana's heart. Her communication with Pierre has diminished lately, yet she feels obligated to at least tell him that she is with someone else now. She has fond memories of their Paris affair, and she was genuinely happy with Pierre while it lasted. So she decides to write him the traditional "Dear John" letter of breaking up in e-mail form. Unexpectedly, Pierre does not take it badly. He wishes Diana happiness, and he tells her that it is for the best since he cannot offer her marriage because he is not yet ready to give up his bachelorhood. He adds that the new man in her life is fortunate to have her. Diana has always known what a good man Pierre is, and she feels lucky to have known him intimately.

Athena observes that Diana is a changed woman when she drops by their parents' home. She chances upon Diana in the kitchen helping their mom, something she did not do before. Athena does not readily respond when Diana asks her how she is because she is unprepared. It is not

Diana's nature to inquire about her well-being. Another unexpected behavior from Diana.

"Diana is moving out of here," Marina shares with Athena in Diana's presence.

"Oh, where to?," Athena inquires.

"Somewhere downtown for proximity reasons where it's more convenient for work," Diana clarifies.

Actually, Diana has decided to move in with Paolo. He has acquired a place downtown for them. He tells her that he is giving up his room at the hotel because he has no more need for it.

"No more hiding. Now I can show you off to everybody," he states.

"So it was your place of rendezvous with your girlfriends?" Diana wants to know, with a trace of jealousy in her voice.

"Yes, but that was before you came into my life. You should not feel jealous because now there's only you, *amore*." He hugs her, and she is assuaged.

Diana cannot tell her parents about her living arrangements with Paolo because she knows they are righteous. They will never sanction the modern-day alternative of living-in, and she does not want to hurt them.

—⁓•◦❦◦◦❦◦•⁓—

"Diana is moving in with Paolo at the new place he acquired downtown. He shared the news with me today," Jon advises Athena.

"So that's where she's going. She told the family when I was there that she's moving somewhere downtown for proximity reasons, without really elaborating."

"He's also going to introduce his son Luigi to her this Friday. Paolo is pretty serious with their relationship."

"I'm glad. I hope she is too because I don't want to see him hurt. He appears to be a respectable man."

———⁓⁓⊙⊙⊙⁓⁓———

Paolo picks up Luigi at the condo, and his son is excited to see him. He introduces him to Diana, and Luigi immediately warms up to her. He rattles off about his toys and school to Diana, while Paolo listens with satisfaction. He is a precocious and inquisitive five-year-old. Diana realizes that it makes her a stepmother, and she likes it. She sees Paolo in Luigi, and they have the same eyes, so Luigi is an extension of her affection for Paolo.

Diana does not mind sharing Paolo with his son since she has Paolo for the entire week, and Luigi has only the weekend, so she is fine with it. Luigi comments when they arrive at the new place: "Nice place, Papa." Luigi has his own room at the new place which Diana decorated earlier. His face lights up as he sees Diana's handiwork.

Earlier, Diana skimmed through magazines to get ideas. Then she shopped for items for the room which would delight a small boy, like cars and action heroes. She and Paolo even installed a moving toy train in one area of the room. She decided on red, white, and blue for the colors of the room.

"Cool!," Luigi keeps repeating as he surveys his new room.

"Diana prepared this for you," Paolo reveals to his son. Luigi runs to Diana and hugs her.

"Thank you," Luigi tells her. She cannot explain her feelings for this adorable boy, who is of Paolo's genes, and now she feels is part of her.

Their weekend is spent going out to eat, swimming in the pool, and watching a kid's movie. Luigi loves to eat at *Paolo's* because he knows his father cooked the food, especially his favorite *bolognese* pasta. Paolo notes that Luigi is usually sad when it is time for him to return to the condo. Paolo knows in his heart that it is only because Luigi loves him and wants to be with him.

"Will you be here when I visit again?," Luigi asks Diana.

"Of course, Luigi, I will always be here. I'll see you next time, okay? We'll have fun together."

"I like Diana, Papa," he tells his father as Paolo brings him back to the condo.

"Me too, son." Paolo hopes that his former wife will remarry and give Luigi to him permanently.

CHAPTER 31

Doubts

Athena knocks off early from work on a weekday to shop for a birthday gift for Faith, one of her writers. She walks along the sidewalk coming from her office, and passes by Starbucks, then suddenly she freezes. Through the glass, she spots Jon sitting in one of the tables having coffee with a blond woman. She knows Jon's profile unmistakably. The woman is facing the street, and Athena can see her looking at him with a big smile on her face. She does not recognize the woman, but from a distance, she is obviously pretty. Athena is shaken by the scene and remains immobile. She soon recovers and hurries away confused.

When she reaches home, she seeks refuge in her bedroom and breaks into tears. After a while, when her disturbed emotion subsides, she calls Barbara because she needs to talk to someone. She relates what she saw.

"I can't believe it, Barbs. Do you think he's being unfaithful to me?"

"Let's not jump into conclusions, Athena. It may be a client or even a relative."

"The thing is he didn't mention to me that he's meeting someone. I can't help but suspect."

"Maybe he forgot, or it could be a spur-of-the-moment thing. I want to give him the benefit of the doubt. I like Jon, and he doesn't strike me as someone who will betray you."

"I'm hurt, Barbs. I love him very much, but I can't accept infidelity. You know that."

"You're not sure about that. What do you plan to do now? Are you going to confront him, or wait until he tells you?"

"I'm inclined to wait for him to tell me. What if he doesn't? Won't that make him guilty of hiding something from me? I'm scared, Barbs."

"Think positive, Athena. If Jon intends to do something wrong, he will do it clandestinely, and not choose Starbucks where he is in plain view."

"Sorry, Barbs, it's hard to think straight when I'm feeling like this. I just don't want to be hurt again."

"I understand. I know in my heart that Jon will not hurt you. It's obvious how crazy he is about you. Angelo and I have observed that."

"You think so?"

"I believe so. He has eyes only for you, Athena. We witnessed that ourselves. You have to calm down. I have a strong feeling Jon is going to call you soon."

"Thanks, Barbs. You're a real friend."

"Call me later. I want to know what happens."

———⚬⚬⚬———

At 6:00 p.m., Athena's phone rings. It's Jon calling. *Barbara is right about predicting Jon's call.*

"Hi, sweetheart. I called your office, but I was told you left early. Are you home?"

"Yes, I'm home now, Jon."

"Is something wrong? You sound different. Are you sick?"

"No, I'm okay."

"May I go over and see you now? I miss you already."

"I'll wait for you, Jon."

Athena freshens up and nervously anticipates Jon's arrival. She is on edge, and the doorbell startles her. The minute she opens the door, Jon envelops her in his arms.

"I miss you, darling. How are you?" He looks down at her. He does not detect that she has been crying after she applied some make-up to conceal it. He takes her hand and they sit on the sofa.

"I've been wanting to call you the whole day, but I was deluged with work. Then towards afternoon, a lady acquaintance of mine made an urgent request to see me about some documents for a property she and her husband are acquiring. I suggested a quick meeting at Starbucks so we could have coffee. There went my day," he says in frustration.

"Oh, Jon." She snuggles up to him, and a teardrop falls.

"Hey, what's wrong, darling? Are you crying?" He tilts her chin and wipes away the single teardrop from her cheek. His expression shows real concern for her.

"I'm fine now, Jon. Give me a minute to breathe." She takes a deep breath, looks at him, and continues.

"I saw you this afternoon with a blond woman when I passed by Starbucks, and immediately it hit me that something was wrong because you didn't mention that meeting to me. Different thoughts ran into my head."

"Athena, my darling, are you worried I'd be unfaithful to you?" He laughs.

"Please don't laugh at me."

"I can't help it, love, because I find it ridiculous. I'll never do that to you. I promise. So banish such thoughts from your mind." He kisses her tenderly, and she relaxes in his arms. *How can I not love this man?*

"Lissa is a friend, and we used to date, but she's happily married now. It wasn't a planned meeting, and she just wanted my advice."

"Sorry, Jon, for doubting you. I've been hurt before, and I don't want to go through that again. I love you very much."

"I love you too, more than you know, and there's no other woman but you. C'mon, let's go somewhere and have dinner."

Later she gets an I-told-you-so reaction from Barbara.

CHAPTER 32

Shopping

Jon receives a phone call from his sister Marianne in Washington, D.C.

"Hi, Jon. Mom is turning 60 on Saturday and we're planning a dinner for her with the family. She has no idea yet about our plan. Can you come here? We want you to be the big surprise."

"That's a week from now. Okay, I'll arrange my trip. How can you hide it from her, Marianne? Mom is very perceptive."

"We'll tell her that we're treating her out on her birthday so she won't suspect anything. Robert, Claire, and their two kids are coming from Baltimore. She's used to having them here since they're not far from where we are, but she rarely sees you, so I'm sure she'll be thrilled, Jon."

"I miss Mom, Marianne. I wish I could see her more often. I'll book my flight and hotel reservation now."

"The affair is in the evening, so you can arrive here Saturday morning."

"I want to spend time with her. I can reserve Sunday for our bonding time, then maybe return here early on Monday. I don't want to be away too long because I'll miss my girlfriend," he says with a chuckle.

"My goodness, Jon, you must really love her. Do you plan to marry her?"

"Definitely. I'll let you know very soon."

As he gets off the phone, Jon asks Amanda to book him a round-trip ticket to Washington, D.C. She makes a hotel reservation for him at the Jefferson Hotel, which is a small historic hotel with a great view. Jon has stayed there before, and he likes its ambience.

———

"I'm leaving on Saturday for Washington, D.C to be at my mom's 60th birthday. My sister called and said that they're organizing a family dinner for her. I'm supposed to be the big surprise since she rarely sees me," Jon relates to Athena.

"That's wonderful, Jon. Enjoy your family. I'll surely miss you."

"I'll miss you too. I won't be there long, and will be back on Monday. Will you help me choose a birthday gift for Mom?"

"Sure, Jon. What's you mom like to help us decide what to get her?"

"Oh, she's vain and loves to dress well."

"How about getting her accessories, like a bracelet or earrings?"

"That's fine. Let's go shopping later."

They visit a few jewelry stores and take a look at the pieces on display. Jon decides to buy his mom diamond earrings. They find an exquisite pair at Tiffany & Co.

with a fine setting, and comes with authentication papers. Jon reveals that his mom does not wear huge jewelry, so this one, in Athena's assessment, is just the right and conservative size. However, she thinks the price is too steep, but Jon does not mind. He buys it and has the store wrap it.

On the day that Jon departs for Washington, D.C., Athena is already feeling the pangs of loneliness. It is their first separation since they became sweethearts. He has always been around, so now she feels the emptiness. *He will be gone only for a few days,* she convinces herself.

Jon keeps busy with his iPad during the long flight of more than five hours to the state capital, but his thoughts keep drifting to Athena, so he decides to doze off for at least an hour. He realizes that he has never missed a person this much.

Chapter 33

Surprise

Jon contacts Marianne after checking in at his hotel.

"Welcome back to D.C., Jon. Mom doesn't suspect our plan, but a while ago she asked where we're having dinner. By the way, she also asked if you had called. I guess she expects you to call and greet her on her birthday."

"I couldn't do that on the flight. I'll call her now and not mention where I am so she'll think I'm in San Francisco, and she won't be suspicious."

"Hey, Jon, the party is at Dubliner at 7:00. I'll text you when we're all there so you can make your grand entrance. We want it to be a surprise for her."

"Gosh, Marianne, I hope we don't give Mom a heart attack," and they both laugh.

Jon immediately calls up his mom.

"Happy Birthday, Mom! How are you feeling on your special day?"

"Jonathan, it's you! Thank you for remembering my birthday. I've been expecting your call. I thought you had forgotten because you usually call early."

"How can I forget your birthday, Mom? Not in a million years. Are you going to have a grand celebration? Turning 60 is a milestone."

"Oh, just dinner with the family. I wish you were here with us, Jonathan."

"I try to be when I can, Mom."

"Are you working hard, son?"

"No, Mom. Besides, it's Saturday today."

"I know, but you're already a successful lawyer, so there's no need for you to work hard."

"Okay, Mom, I'll take your advice. Well, enjoy your dinner, and say hello for me to the family. I love you, Mom, and Happy Birthday again."

"Thanks, Jonathan. I love you too, son."

Jon has time on his hands before the dinner event. He strolls along the city's commercial area and visits the shops. He enters a bookstore and browses through the titles. He purchases a copy of *A New Earth* by Eckhart Tolle for Athena. He read favorable reviews on it, and he knows she loves to read. He also gets her a bottle of perfume of a floral bouquet, which he thinks she will appreciate. He picks an angel figurine for Amanda's collection.

It is still early when he gets back to the hotel, so he takes a swim in the pool, and does three laps. Back in his room, he e-mails Athena.

Hi, my darling Athena,

How are you holding up without me? I'm joking since I'm the one who is really lonely and missing you a lot. I miss kissing and hugging you. You're so much a part of me now that I don't feel complete without you.

The surprise party for Mom is tonight at Dubliner. My sister Marianne will text me when they're already all there so I can make my entrance and surprise Mom. I'll tell you about it later.
Take care, and remember that you're the only one for me.

Much love,
Jon

Jon's e-mail touches Athena's heart. She misses him so much that on their first night of separation, she struggles with her loneliness. She replies right away.

Dearest Jon,

I feel lost without you. Do you know that this is our first separation? I miss you so much that I find myself thinking of you all the time. Last night I cried myself to sleep. I feel you're part of me too.

Enjoy your mom's surprise party and the company of your family. Get back soon.

I love you,
Athena

Athena's e-mail buoys up Jon's spirit. Afterwards, Marianne sends a text to him saying that the family are now all in Dubliner's private room. He has been waiting nearby inconspicuously. As Jon opens the door to the function room, everyone's eyes are focused on him, and his mom is the most surprised person in the room.

"Happy Birthday, Mom." He hands her his gift and hugs her.

"Jonathan, this is the biggest surprise of my life! I didn't expect you to be here. I thought you were calling from San Francisco."

"I couldn't tell you, Mom, or else I'd spoil the surprise."

"You naughty boy. Well, it worked, and you really surprised me. We're all happy you're here with us, son. Marianne, did you plan this?"

"We all did, Mom," Marianne responds.

Jon bonds with his siblings and in-laws, and enjoys teasing his nephew and nieces. His brother Robert has a son and a daughter, and Marianne has one daughter. They savor Dubliner's food, which is a fusion of American, European, and Irish cuisines. The family continue to interact until late in the evening. They are glad that they made their mom's birthday special for her.

"Tomorrow is your day with me, Mom. It will be our bonding time," Jon announces.

"I'll look forward to it, Jonathan."

<hr>

Jon takes his mom to a Mexican restaurant for lunch since she has a liking for Mexican food. They have *enchiladas*, *burritos,* and *tacos.* He tells her about his work and she listens with rapt attention. She is even interested to hear about the details of his court cases. He talks about Athena and confesses to his mom that he misses her, then shows her Athena's photo.

"She's lovely, darling."

"She is, Mom, inside and out. You'll like her. She helped me choose the earrings for you."

She thanks Jon for the diamond earrings, which she is wearing to show him that she appreciates his gift. They have coffee after their heavy meal and spend longer hours just talking. Dinner is barbecue at Marianne's place with her husband Daryl manning the grill. Jon experiences a little sadness saying goodbye to his family, especially his mom, who is very grateful for his coming to her birthday.

When he returns to his hotel room, he shoots off another e-mail to Athena.

My darling Athena,

The surprise party for Mom was a success. She was indeed surprised to see me. She loves the earrings. It was great seeing my siblings and their families.

Today was my bonding time with Mom. I treated her to her favorite Mexican food, and we talked long about my work and about you.

I can't wait to get back to you, kiss and embrace you. I miss you, darling.

Much love,
Jon

Athena replies to his e-mail without delay. *He told his mom about me?*

Dearest Jon,

Thanks for sharing the accounts of your mom's birthday. I'm glad you were able to be there for it and see your family.

It was a lonely weekend for me. I can't tell you how much I miss you, and I long to be in your arms again.

I love you very much,
Athena

Jon's flight is very early, and arrives in San Francisco after sunrise. He proceeds to Athena's condo and surprises her as she is preparing to go to work. He takes her into his arms and kisses her long until she is out of breath.

"I couldn't wait to do this," he admits, and she is at a loss for words.

Chapter 34

Investments

Dwight Johnson, one of the senior partners, asked Jon to handle a celebrated case related to the so-called Ponzi scheme. Their client is Peter Trench, who invested $3 billion with George E. Swann Investment Securities. Following the Bernie Madoff fiasco, Swann defrauded its investors, mostly big-time, of their money. Jon's initial step is to gather his team of two lawyers and give a short lecture on the mechanics of the Ponzi scheme. He includes Amanda since she will be doing the paperwork, and he also wants her to have a better understanding of it. Jon begins his lecture.

"You may already be familiar with the Ponzi scheme. I'll explain it further. What and who is Ponzi? Well, it originated from a man named Charles Ponzi who became noted for this kind of scam in 1920. Today the Ponzi scheme is synonymous with fraudulent investment operation."

"An investment one makes is supposed to be receiving dividends from the profits earned, right? That's not how it works with the Ponzi scheme. Here, the investment company pays the investor from other investors' money or from the investor's own money, which was just deposited in the bank and not actually invested."

"The investor's money, therefore, does not earn a profit, and the investment company just juggles the funds. It entices investors by offering as much as 21% yearly interest. If you invested a large sum of money, that would translate into millions in interest and dividends alone. These fraudulent investment companies are good at their game. They make the investors believe that their money is put into a high-yield investment program and offshore investment, which may sound quite convincing."

"That's what our client, Peter Trench, got himself into. What happens is that later on their scam catches up with them, and they can no longer pay their investors. This is what happened to Bernie Madoff, who is now serving a 150-year prison term for defrauding hundreds of investors."

"We're talking about billions of dollars here. Trench wants his money back. That's $3 billion. He's just one of them, and there are other rich guys who invested even more. So you can imagine the amount of money involved. I'll need you to research thoroughly on this for our client's sake. Let's trace the transactions and get hold of all the records."

"Is George E. Swann Investment Securities registered with the Securities and Exchange Commission?," one of the lawyers wants to know.

"I already checked that out, and it's not registered. Investment companies like this are usually not registered with the SEC. That's one thing to take note of," Jon replies.

"Feel free to approach me if you have any more questions or if you need clarification. Let's work on this together," Jon adds.

"Thanks, JP, for including me in the lecture. Honestly, I was in the dark before about this Ponzi scheme," Amanda admits.

"Well, you learned something today, Amanda. We should all be aware of this. You can also become a victim of the pyramid scheme, which is of a smaller proportion, so be careful because it can be a painful experience to lose your hard-earned money. It's a common occurrence, and it can happen to any of us. People are easily lured into it because of hard times."

"I'll take note of that, JP."

———

Jon usually shares his day with Athena, and she does the same for him. She admits that she does not know much about the Ponzi scheme, so Jon explains it to her.

"Where do you put your savings?," he asks her.

"In the bank. I feel it's safer there."

"Investment houses offer higher returns, but if you decide to invest in one of them, check it out first if it's a reputable company, and if it's listed with the SEC."

"Thanks for the valuable advice, Mr. Lawyer. I appreciate it," giving him a peck on the cheek.

———

Jon and his team do not lose time in working on the Trench case. They do extensive research and analyze all the records. By now the remaining assets of the George E. Swann Investment Securities are in government hands, and the liquidation of assets is assigned to the Securities Investment Protection Corporation (SIPC) through the Securities Investment Protection Act (SIPA). There are other lawsuits filed by wealthy investors, so Jon's team knows it has to act fast before the money runs out.

Jon files their claim with SIPC online, and continues to follow it up through e-mail and phone calls to his contacts in Washington, D.C. In less than a month, Peter Trench got his money back.

CHAPTER 35

Abduction

"Paolo, Luigi is missing! I don't know what happened. He was not on the school bus today." Natalia is in a state of panic on the phone.

"What? How did that happen?," Paolo practically shouts.

"I don't know. He was supposed to arrive here at noon, but when l went down to meet the school bus, he wasn't on it. The driver said he didn't notice him board the bus."

"Did you call the school?"

"Yes, I did, but they confirmed that he's not there either".

"How about the police?"

"Not yet. I decided to call you first."

"I'll take care of it. Stay next to the phone in case there are calls."

Paolo is frantic and deeply worried, not knowing what to do first. His mind is on his son, and he prays that he is all right. He decides to contact Jon.

"Jon, my son Luigi is missing. He didn't come home from school today. Natalia said the school told her that he's not there either. Tell me what I should do. Should I contact the police?"

"Let's hope it's not a case of ransom, Paolo. I'll call the police for you. I know Detective Russo. I'll get back to you."

"Thanks, Jon. I appreciate this."

Right after Paolo ends his call, another call comes in on his mobile phone, and he does not recognize the number. He has the impression that the caller is trying to disguise his voice by an octave.

"Mr. Romano, I have your son. You will get him back unharmed if you pay me $5 million. Listen carefully. I don't want any police involvement. If you contact the police, your son will die. Get that, Mr. Romano?"

"I'll follow your instructions. I'll do anything. Please just don't hurt my son," Paolo pleads, and he is sweating from fear. "Is my son with you now? May I talk to him?"

"Okay, but just for a few seconds."

Paolo hears Luigi's voice on the phone. "Papa, come and get me."

"Yes, Luigi, I will come for you. Just wait for me. Be a brave boy, okay? Are you all right?"

"That's enough, Mr. Romano," the abductor interrupts. "I'll call you back in an hour to tell you where we will meet. In an hour, is that clear? Remember my warning about police involvement. You have plenty of time to withdraw the money from the bank," and the phone goes dead. Paolo immediately calls Jon.

"Jon, your hunch is right. Luigi has been kidnapped," he reports, agitated. "I got a call from his abductor, who's demanding $5 million for Luigi. He warned me against informing the police. He'll call back after an hour to give instructions for the drop-off."

"It's still best to let the police in on it, Paolo. Detective Russo already knows. They can handle this discreetly. It is important that they catch this abductor. Do you have any suspect as to who knows you have the money to pay such a ransom?"

"I have no idea, Jon. Natalia knows, of course. Luigi goes to St. Augustine School, which is an expensive school with ample security, so I don't know how the abductor got to him without being detected."

"If you're in the restaurant right now, I suggest you stay there. Detective Russo and his men may want to be present when that call comes."

"I'm now in my office in the first restaurant downtown."

"I'll call Detective Russo right now. I'll go there too.

In a matter of minutes, Detective Russo and two of his men arrive at the restaurant, and Jon follows. They decide they do not need to trace the abductor's call since he will already identify the drop-off point. They suspect he is not a professional, and this may even be his first job. He also seems to be in a hurry to get his hands on the ransom money.

"Should I withdraw the money now from the bank, Detective?," Paolo inquires.

"There may not be any need for that, Mr. Romano. He'll ask to see the money, so we can make sure the top bills are real. This guy doesn't sound like he has experience in this, and he may even be working alone. We believe he's playing on your fear of losing your son."

Detective Russo advises Paolo on what to do. "Mr. Romano, don't agree to hand over the bag right away. Get hold of your son first before anything else."

After exactly one hour, Paolo's mobile phone rings. The abductor gives him instructions to go to the Japanese Tea Garden at the Golden Gate Bridge Park, the site he indicates for the exchange. He sets the meeting time at 7:00 p.m. He reminds Paolo again about the no-police presence.

"We'll surround the place. We'll go there early, and he won't even know we're there," Detective Russo assures a tense Paolo.

In the meantime, Paolo calls Natalia and Diana to recount Luigi's plight. Both women are full of concern.

CHAPTER 36

For Luigi's Sake

Paolo drives alone to the Golden Gate Bridge Park and arrives at the Japanese Tea Garden at 6:45 p.m. He keeps asking himself, *What will I do if something bad happens to Luigi, my flesh and blood*? After alighting from the vehicle, he takes the bag of "money" from inside the car, then stands in front of the building and waits. He does not detect the presence of the police and Jon with them, but he knows they are there somewhere.

After a short while, a man wearing a baseball cap suddenly appears from the right side of the building, holding Luigi by the hand and what looks like a gun in his other hand. Luigi instantly shouts "Papa" and wants to get away from the guy, but his abductor holds on to him like a vise, so he starts to cry.

"It's okay, Luigi. Papa is here. Don't cry, son," Paolo says in a comforting tone.

"Open the bag, Mr. Romano," the abductor orders him. Paolo moves closer and unzips the bag to reveal its contents. The abductor peers at the contents for a few seconds, and he seems satisfied.

"Okay, toss it to me now."

"Oh, no. You give me my son first or you won't get your money," Paolo states firmly.

The abductor can see that Paolo is serious and is not about to give in, so he obliges after a moment's hesitation in his eagerness to get hold of the bag. He lets go of Luigi, who runs to his father's arms. Then the police close in on the startled abductor, who is surrounded by a team of armed policemen.

"Drop the gun," Detective Russo orders, and the abductor has no choice but to follow.

"Thank you, Jon. Thanks to you, Detective Russo, and your men," Paolo expresses his gratitude. "Who is this guy?," he asks while referring to the now- handcuffed abductor.

"That's Roger, Papa," Luigi answers.

"Do you know him, Luigi?" Paolo appears surprised at Luigi's admission.

"Yes, he's Mama's friend."

"Did he hurt you?"

"No, Papa."

"Thank God, son."

Upon hearing Luigi's testimony, Detective Russo decides to investigate further. He and his men want to know if Paolo's ex is involved in the kidnapping scheme. They discover that Roger is indeed Natalia's current boyfriend. They question Natalia, and afterwards are convinced that she had no knowledge about the abduction, and had no inkling about Roger's malicious plan. Natalia is disheartened upon learning that her boyfriend planned the abduction, and breaks up with him. She does not want to have anything to do with him after the incident.

The police and Jon conclude that Roger must have gathered information about Paolo's wealth. He was interested in Natalia because he was aware she has money, but he realized he could get more from Paolo, so he devised a plan to kidnap Luigi.

———————

Luigi's abduction opens doors for Paolo to file for full custody. Jon points this out to him.

"Your son's safety is of utmost importance, isn't it?," Jon suggests.

"Of course, Jon. I went through hell when he was abducted. I love my son very much."

"You can petition the court for custody and work it out so Luigi can stay with you permanently. Natalia can still have visitation rights. After what happened, he'll be safer with you. Does he get along with Diana?"

"They get along very well. He always looks for her in his every visit. Diana decorated his room, and he loves it. Thanks for suggesting it, Jon. You really are the best lawyer."

———————

Knowing Natalia's temperament, Paolo suggests to Jon that they should tread carefully to avoid a battle with her. She may present some resistance if she senses that Paolo wants Luigi with him.

"In that case, it may not be a good idea to surprise her with a petition. Perhaps we should warn her beforehand, Paolo. What do you think?"

"You mean, like talk to her first?"

"Why not? Maybe we can make her understand why you want Luigi to live with you. I can do that for you even without your presence."

"Okay, I'll go with that. Just be careful, Jon. Natalia has a fiery temper. When do you plan to do this?"

"As soon as possible. I'll ask her to see me."

—⁓⁓⁓⁓⁓—

Natalia agrees to see Jon at his office. She arrives alone without her lawyer. She appears comfortable talking to Jon since the divorce because she is grateful to him for giving her a good settlement, which she did not anticipate. She knows that the lawyer has a hand in these things, and she finds Jon easy to talk to. She seems to be in a good mood when they meet.

"Good morning, Natalia. How are you? Thank you for coming."

"I'm fine, thank you. What is this about, Mr. Prentiss?"

"Call me Jon. Have a seat." After they settle in their seats, Jon proceeds with his suggestion with care.

"It's really about Luigi. You and Paolo love your son, and I know that his safety is important to both of you. After the abduction attempt by your ex-boyfriend, we got to thinking that it can happen again, and we don't want that. So I'm suggesting that you allow Luigi to stay with Paolo where he's safer."

"You mean permanently? What about me, Jon?," she starts to protest.

"I have you in mind too, Natalia. You can have unlimited visitation rights because Paolo wants Luigi to be in touch with his mother. Paolo will assign a bodyguard to be with him when he's with you. This will free you from worrying about Luigi's safety. Paolo has only good intentions for Luigi. That sounds fair, doesn't it? It's really for Luigi's sake, Natalia." She ponders on Jon's suggestion.

"Can Luigi visit me often?"

"Of course. That's actually up to you. Paolo will allow it. You're Luigi's biological mother, and he respects that. What is of vital importance to him is Luigi's well-being. I can assure you that Paolo has no selfish motives. His only concern is Luigi. This is motivated purely to protect your boy. Well, are you amenable to it?"

"I suppose I can agree to your suggestion. It sounds like the right thing to do for Luigi."

"You have a smart boy, Natalia, and we're doing this for him."

Paolo files a petition for full custody in court through Jon's law firm. With the expressed agreement of the mother, the judge approved it without question. Luigi immediately moves in with his father, and Paolo cannot be any happier. Paolo hires a bodyguard to be with Luigi during the day, and even accompany him to and from school.

CHAPTER 37

The Proposal

Jon decides it is time he proposes to Athena. He has no doubt in his mind that she is the woman he wants as his wife. He secretly solicits the help of Barbara in choosing the right engagement ring. For the entire week, he has been elated and excited over the prospect of finally marrying the love of his life. Amanda, who is also assisting him in his plan, hears him often singing in his office.

He considers a number of venue options to guarantee that it is going to be a romantic setting. He wants it to be a memorable event for Athena, one she will never forget. He narrows it down to three choices: Golden Gate Bridge or the park, Luxury Catamaran Sailing Cruise, and Twin Peaks. He asks Amanda for her opinion. She favors the Sailing Cruise, which is a slow trip along the San Francisco Bay, passing under the Golden Gate Bridge, circling the Alcatraz, and sailing by Sausalito. It has a sheltered cabin if Jon chooses to make his proposal there.

"They actually all provide a romantic setting. The Golden Gate Bridge is a San Francisco landmark, and the

Twin Peaks have a spectacular view of the city, and can be very romantic at sunset," Amanda tells him. "However, the Sailing Cruise is a relaxing trip and perhaps offers a bit more privacy. You may not want people gawking at you when you kneel down on one knee, JP."

"You're right there, Amanda. This is my moment with Athena, and I want it to be just right. Can you find out what is the least crowded day for the cruise? The less people, the better."

"I'll call them and find out. Gee, I'm as excited as you are, JP. Athena is a very lucky girl."

"That's not all I have in mind, Amanda. I want to hire that plane which writes messages in the sky. Can you find out about that?"

"What kind of messages, JP?"

"I want the message '*Marry Me, Athena*' written in the sky while we're cruising along San Francisco Bay so she'll see it."

"Great idea, JP. What can be more romantic than that? I'll arrange it. It should be properly timed while you're at sea. How exciting!"

When Jon mentions the cruise to Athena, she does not suspect anything. She thinks Jon just wants to get away from the tedium of work and have some quiet time with her. Amanda makes reservations for the 3:00 p.m. trip the following Monday, a not-too-popular day. Athena is looking forward to it, wanting to spend a leisurely time with Jon and enjoy his company. They leave work early, ensuring that they don thick-enough clothing since it can be cold at sea.

On board, they experience peace as they view the San Francisco skyline from afar and watch the many white sailboats dotting the Bay. The Golden Gate Bridge is still majestic seeing it from below. Alcatraz appears massive, and the boats moored in Sausalito are a sight to behold. A few sea lions are honking nearby.

"This is lovely, Jon. I'm glad you thought of doing this. It frees us from the din of the crowded city even for a short time," Athena admits as they look out to sea, with Jon hugging her from behind. She loves the feeling of closeness with him.

"I like being with you like this. Let's find ways of enjoying each other in this manner away from our busy existence." He kisses her cheek. "Hmm, you smell good, you always do." Then he takes her hand.

"Come, let's go down to the cabin and have something to drink," he leads her below. "What would you like to drink? Do you want something to eat?," he asks.

"I'm not hungry. Just soda maybe."

He orders soda for them and they find seats. Then they hear soft music waft into the cabin, and it is playing "*The Way You Look Tonight*". Jon glances at Athena with a meaningful expression on his face.

"Let's dance," he invites her.

"Jon, nobody is dancing," she cautions him, referring to the sparse crowd in the sheltered cabin.

"That's okay. We won't occupy much space." He takes her hand, and they dance in a tight embrace within their small circle. Two senior couples soon follow suit and dance too.

"We don't have a theme song as a couple. What do you say about having this as our theme song since this is an important moment for us?," he suggests.

"I like it. It's really appropriate because this song was played in the movie "*My Best Friend's Wedding*" while they were dancing on a cruise much like this."

"We have the right theme song then." He leads her back to her seat. He takes both her hands in his and looks deeply into her eyes for a long time.

"What?," Athena asks. "Why are you looking at me like that, Jon?"

"Do you know how much I love you?"

"I love you too, Jon."

"I want to be with you forever, Athena." He suddenly hears the drone of a small plane overhead just as Amanda's text comes in telling him to look up to the sky.

"Come, let's go up. I have something to show you," he says to Athena and leads her by the hand. As they reach the top, they notice the passengers on the catamaran looking up to the sky smiling, and Athena follows their gaze. The message '*Marry Me, Athena*' written in the sky is very visible to all of them. Athena gapes at it, then at Jon. He grins widely at her.

"Jon, is this your doing?"

"What do you think? How many Athenas are there?," throwing back at her the comment she made to him before. "Yes, darling, it's my message for you."

He then produces a small black box from his pocket and goes down on one knee, and Athena continues to gape at him. "Will you marry me, Athena?"

"Jon, this is a total surprise!," putting one hand over her somersaulting heart.

"I really wanted it to be a surprise."

"You never gave me any hint that you're going to propose. I don't know what to say."

"Please say 'yes', darling," he implores.

"Yes, yes! *So this is what he meant by the important moment*, she realizes.

He rises and takes the perfect three-carat diamond ring from its box and slips it into her finger, then lifts her bodily and swings her in his embrace while kissing her. The passengers on board are too busy gazing at the message written in the sky that they hardly notice Jon's proposal. The newly engaged couple continues to hug and kiss, heedless of the other people there, until the catamaran docks. They are both in a daze as they disembark, still reeling from his proposal. They go to Pier 39 to browse and take a leisurely stroll, his arm over her shoulder and hers on his waist, before having a quiet dinner there, constantly looking into each other's eyes and relishing their new status as an engaged couple.

Afterwards, Jon texts Barbara and Amanda with the message, 'Done. It was perfect. Thanks.' Athena discovers that Barbara helped in choosing the ring, and they talk for an hour on the phone. Athena related everything to her excitedly, and she is bathed with joy over the day's event.

CHAPTER 38

Announcement

At the office of Coalition on Homelessness the following Saturday, Jon and Athena wait for Rodrigo. They approach him as he arrives.

"Hi, Dad," Athena greets him with a kiss.

"Good morning, Mr. Bravo, may I have a word with you?," Jon says.

"Good morning, Jon. Sure."

"I asked Athena to be my wife, and she said 'yes'. May I have your blessing, sir?"

"That's wonderful news! Congratulations to both of you. Of course, you have my blessing, Jon."

"Thank you, Mr. Bravo. I know this is such an informal setting."

"That's all right, Jon. This is good enough. I'm happy for both of you."

"Thank you, Dad." Athena hugs Rodrigo.

"I can make the announcement during your Mom's birthday, Athena. She'll be turning 50 soon and I'm going to honor her with a party. The announcement of your engagement will be our big surprise for her."

"That's great, Dad. Let me know how I can help."

"It's all planned. Your Mom's two sisters are taking care of it."

—⟳⟳⟳⟳⟳⟳⟳—

The venue of Marina's 50th birthday party is her sister's spacious home. The guests are her siblings and their families, the Bravos, and John. Her two younger sisters handle all the preparations. The tables are laid out in the wide living room and extend into the *lanai*. Each table has a colorful floral arrangement decorated with ribbons. When Marina arrives with Rodrigo, she admires her sisters' creation and thanks them.

"If turning 50 is as nice as this, I don't mind getting old," she lets her sisters know.

Athena arrives with Jon, and she introduces him to her relatives. They are eyeing him, being a stranger among them. She is in a pink lace dress which brings out her femininity. Diana makes a late appearance when everybody has already arrived. She wears a short and sexy metallic grey outfit, the usual type of attire she is identified with. The twins are endowed with shapely, long legs, and unlike Athena, Diana loves to show hers off.

Diana instantly spots Jon because he is tall and stands in the crowd. He is talking to Gabriel, a lawyer like him and the husband of one of Marina's sisters, and Diana goes near him.

"Hi, Jon. I didn't expect to see you here."

"Hi, Diana. I'm here for a reason."

"Let's go, Jon. Our table is waiting for us," Gabriel interrupts and leads him to their table, so the conversation is interrupted. Diana cannot stop from wondering why Jon is present in her mother's birthday party. *Jon said he is here for a reason.* The only reason she can think of is something legal or related to a case. He is talking animatedly to her Uncle Gabriel, who is also a lawyer. She frowns as she sees Athena seated next to Jon, but she still does not suspect anything since their other single female cousins are also at the same table.

The dinner, conversations, and laughing go on. Marina is apparently pleased, and enjoying her party. After dessert, Rodrigo rises from his seat and goes to the front.

"Thank you all for being here to honor Marina on her 50th birthday," he addresses the guests. He then faces Marina. "Happy Birthday, my beloved wife! Marina, you don't look a day older than 30. I love you even more now than when we were first married." Laughter ensues from the relatives. "I hope you're happy with the turnout of your birthday. I thank your two lovely sisters for making this possible. It only proves how much they love you, just as our daughters and I do. We only want you to be happy, you know that. To make you even happier on your birthday, I have a very special announcement. I know this will make you smile." He pauses for a few seconds.

"I would like to announce the engagement of our daughter Athena to Jonathan Prentiss." The relatives clapped and cheered. "Jon, Athena, please come forward." Jon leads Athena by the hand to where Rodrigo stands. The relatives cheer even louder. Athena hugs her Dad and Mom, who are both beaming with joy, and Jon shakes Rodrigo's hand and hugs Marina. Diana is peeved with the announcement. *Athena is Jon's girlfriend? Why did I not know this?*, she accuses herself. Jon gives Athena a kiss and draws her close to him, and it is like a slap in Diana's face.

Diana wants to escape from the party in her disgust, but she is egged by her compulsion to ask Jon a question, and she is curious to know his answer. She finds the opportunity to corner him when she spots him alone for a brief moment. Athena notices her accost Jon.

"Jon, just one question."

"Okay, Diana."

"Did you know all this time that I'm Athena's twin sister?"

"Yes."

"Then why didn't you mention it to me?"

"Those are two questions. Anyway, I'll answer you. It's inappropriate for a lawyer to discuss his personal life with his clients. I have no business telling my clients about details of my relationship. I consider you a client."

"Oh, am I?"

"Let's leave it at that. Don't take it badly, Diana, because I had no malicious intention of keeping my relationship with Athena from you. No offense meant. I hope you're satisfied with my answers. Good night, Diana."

"Don't worry about it. Everything is okay," Jon assures Athena as he relates to her his conversation with Diana. His tight embrace always allays her doubts or fears.

CHAPTER 39

Repercussions

The announcement of Jon and Athena's engagement attracts mixed reactions. Their families and friends are happy for them, except Diana. The news reaches the newspapers and earns a space in their people segment since Jon is a successful lawyer and one of San Francisco's most eligible bachelors. Jon and Athena are not prepared for the magnitude of the after-effects of the announcement as congratulatory greetings pour in. They do not consider themselves celebrities, so it is an unexpected outcome for them. Jon's main concern is Athena. He wants to protect her from any form of publicity.

Jon's and Athena's respective offices are jubilant over the good news. Jon calls his mom, brother, and sister about his engagement. They all congratulate him and promise to attend the wedding.

"My baby is getting married at last! I'm so happy for you, Jonathan," his mom exclaims on the phone.

"Mom, I'm no longer a baby, and it's time that I get married. You'll love Athena. She's a wonderful woman."

"I'm sure she is, son. I know you have good taste when it comes to women."

"Do you know that you have a great influence on me?"

"How nice to hear that from you. I have no idea that you listen to my advice."

"Of course I do, Mom. You're a great mom, and I learned a lot from you."

"Thank you for the acknowledgement, son. Be sure to update us on the wedding plans."

"I will. I love you, Mom."

———

Athena relates to Barbara the seduction attempt of Diana and what she said to Jon, and Barbara reacts with disgust.

"Just as I expected, Athena, but I don't understand why she still tried to tempt Jon when you say she has that chef who loves her."

"Well, maybe she finds Jon attractive, but when she didn't detect a reciprocal admiration from him, she tried seduction, but it didn't work. Thank God. I know that she loves Chef Paolo, but now that she found out that I'm Jon's choice, I suspect she cannot reconcile with the fact that Jon did not yield to her earlier advances. It was a rebuff. There's an explanation to her dagger looks thrown at me during our mom's birthday after the engagement announcement. She doesn't want me to be in a better position than she is. It has always been like that with us. She just cannot accept that someone like Jon would choose me."

"Now I'm worried for you, Athena. Suppose she'll try to hurt you or something? Is she capable of that?"

"I can't really tell you, Barbs, because I don't know what she's capable of."

"Please be careful, won't you?"

———

Diana is fuming mad. Her negative reaction to the engagement is fanned by jealousy. She has always been jealous of Athena. She cannot accept that her twin sister is Jonathan Prentiss' choice for a fiancée, and eventually wife. What she cannot take is that he did not fall for her beauty like the other men in her life, but instead prefers Athena. *What has Athena got that I don't have?* She feels the pain of rejection like a knife thrust into her. She has never felt this unwanted before, and she is not used to defeat. The anger courses through her body, and she trembles from the sheer indignation and emotional upheaval. She keeps asking herself, *Why Athena?*

Athena and Diana may be twins, but they are on opposite poles. Athena is a calm person, and Diana has a temper. Athena has faith in herself, whereas Diana thinks highly of herself and cannot accept that anyone is better than she is, especially her twin. Their parents can see the differences in the twins. What they fail to understand is why there is hardly any similarity between them since they brought them up in the same way, accorded them equal attention, and loved them since infancy to the same degree.

CHAPTER 40

An Attempt

Diana's jealousy consumes her. She cannot think of anything else. Her mind is riveted on raining on Athena's parade. She just cannot acknowledge that Athena has won Jonathan Prentiss' heart. *He is a prize on all counts, and Athena does not deserve him*. She vows to keep Athena from becoming Mrs. Jonathan Prentiss.

Paolo is no stranger to Diana's moods, so when he notices her brooding, he simply leaves her be or takes her into his embrace without speaking. Diana's silence is not new to him, and he does not really mind because he knows he is often not the cause of it. He is always ready to listen to her when her dark mood lifts up. He happens to understand women better than any man because he has been into a lot of relationships with various women. Diana is The Woman for him, and he plans to marry her.

Diana goes out regularly for after-office drinks with the Marketing people. They frequent a popular bar close to their workplace. Three of them are women and two are men this time, and they share a round table.

"What do you do if there's a particular person you don't like whom you don't want to see anymore?," Diana addresses the group.

"Can you not just avoid that person,?" one of the women comments.

"Suppose you can't?," Diana counters.

"There's a better alternative. Eliminate that person," Bob suggests.

"You mean kill the person?," says the other woman, astounded.

"Why not? It's been done before. There are people who do that. Haven't you heard of assassins or hitmen?," Bob explains.

"Have you ever met one before?," Diana asks him.

"Not personally, but I know someone who is in touch with one."

"And who would that be?" Rod, the other guy, is curious to know.

"Do you know George, the bartender over there?" Bob points towards the bar where the bartender is busy pouring drinks. "That's your guy."

"How do you know this, Bob?," Rod questions him.

"Because he helped someone I know get rid of a guy before."

"The assassin didn't get caught by the police?" Diana's curiosity is aroused.

"No. These guys are professionals. They get away with it all the time."

Diana discreetly finds the right opportunity to talk to George. She studies his schedule, when he reports for work, and his free time. She finally gets to talk to him inside a small room behind the bar. She readies her questions, which he answers to her satisfaction. George promises to introduce her to Harry, the assassin, who will carry out the job.

She meets Harry soon after. She learns that his normal fee for a simple elimination job is $10,000 - $5,000 down payment and $5,000 upon completion, and he uses a gun with a silencer. His fee can go higher if the job is more complicated. The following day, Diana meets with Harry behind the bar and hands him the $5,000 down payment plus a photo of Athena. She directs him to where Athena works. He tells Diana that he plans to observe Athena's movements first to decide on the right time to take her.

Diana is filled with anxiety over her "Eliminate Athena" project. She does not tell a soul, and she has no doubt that it is the right alternative. All her life Athena has always been her stumbling block, and she wants to put an end to it once and for all. *I may not have succeeded in seducing Jon, but there's no way Athena can have him,* she decides.

Harry studies Athena's schedule for a week. He observes that she usually leaves their building between 5:00 and 6:00 p.m. He intends to shoot her inconspicuously from behind in the dense afternoon crowd when people are on their way home from work. It is an easy job for him, and he is confident he will go unnoticed. He will just nonchalantly walk away after accomplishing it. To run will create suspicion. Besides, this is not his first job, and he has been successful in the past.

That afternoon, Athena leaves the office before 5:00 p.m. to meet Jon at Starbucks. Harry pretends to read the newspaper in one corner and suddenly straightens up when he spots her as she exits her building, and he immediately tails her. He tries to keep pace with Athena, who is walking briskly. He needs to be right behind her to carry out the job without a snag, and he is sure nobody will even hear the pop of the gun. He is about to take out his gun as he gets closer to Athena when a wayward cyclist rams into him with great force from behind and knocks him down, then sideswipes Athena. She gets sprawled on the sidewalk, and a kind man helps her on her feet. She notices blood oozing from her bruised knee and elbow, and she panics. She is still close to her building, so she walks hurriedly to her office clinic. The doctor and nurse are still there and attend to her injuries. She immediately calls Jon's mobile phone.

Meanwhile, as Harry gets knocked down, two policemen on duty in the neighborhood rush to the scene as he is about to get up with difficulty and obviously dazed from the forceful impact. They find the gun in his possession and a woman's photo with him. They are convinced there is something fishy about it, and whisk him off to the precinct, where he is subjected to questioning.

Jon rushes to the Market Strength clinic and finds Athena there.

"What happened, darling? Are you all right?," Jon asks anxiously.

"I don't know. I felt something hit me from behind and I fell. I'm okay now, Jon."

"It's nothing serious. She's lucky they're just scrapes," the doctor says. "She's free to go now." The doctor had treated her superficial wounds and covered them with band-aid.

"Thank you, doctor," says Athena.

As Jon leads Athena out of the building, they overhear a few men milling around and talking about the recent incident. Jon asks them what happened. They narrate that the police brought the guy hit by the cyclist to the precinct because he had a gun. They suspect he is an assassin since he had the photo of a woman with him.

"What happened to the cyclist? He could have shed light to the incident," Jon tells the men.

"I saw him retrieve his bike and leave in a hurry before the police came. He looked really scared. I figure he wanted to avoid being held responsible for what happened," one of the bystanders offers his opinion.

Then one of them points at Athena.

"She's the woman in the photo. I had a good look at it because I picked it up from the pavement and handed it to the policeman."

Athena trembles, and Jon puts his arms around her.

"Take it easy, darling. I'll take care of this. It's not safe for you to go home right now, so I'll take you to Barbara's place and pass for you later. I'll go to the precinct and follow this up, and maybe they can enlighten me."

CHAPTER 41

Investigation

After dropping off Athena at Barbara's place, Jon proceeds to the precinct. He introduces himself to the Desk Officer and explains his visit.

"I know you, Mr. Prentiss," the officer acknowledges. "I'll take you to the interrogation room so you can listen in from the outside. The suspect is right now being questioned."

John listens to the interrogation through the one-way mirror.

"Harry, you might as well come clean. You already have a bad record with us, and we've been keeping an eye on you. Were you planning to shoot this woman in the photo?," the detective interrogates him, holding up Athena's photo.

"I swear I didn't do anything wrong, detective," Harry replies.

"Then what were you doing with the gun? This is an unlicensed weapon and we can build a case around it as well against you. It even has a silencer, which is used when one wants to muffle the sound of gunfire, like when shooting someone. That's what you were going to do, wasn't it?"

"You're speculating, detective. I'm innocent, I'm telling you. You have nothing against me," Harry raises his voice.

"Don't be arrogant. The street camera has a footage of you taking out your gun right behind this woman in the photo. It's clear you were about to shoot her, Harry. What do you say to that? You can't deny it anymore."

"Are you serious? Harry squirms in his seat.

"Yes, I am. The camera doesn't lie. You're looking at 10 years in jail, Harry, for attempted murder. Do you know that?"

"Even if it wasn't my idea?"

"Start talking. If you tell us who paid you to do it, maybe we can help you and do something about it."

"Okay, okay. I tell you, this woman paid me $10,000 to do it, $5,000 down and $5,000 after the job."

"What woman? What's her name?"

"I don't know her name because she didn't identify herself," he protests.

"Describe her."

As Jon listens to the description of the woman, he feels a coldness sweep over his body. He fears for Athena's life.

———

John is shaken with what he heard at the precinct. He has a glum expression on his face as he gives accounts of the interrogation to Athena, Barbara, and Angelo, feeling as if he is suddenly zapped of energy.

"The assassin was practically describing Diana," he relates to them. He cannot believe that Diana would resort to having Athena killed.

"That's terrible! It's unbelievable that someone wants her sister dead," Barbara comments. Even Angelo has something to say.

"It boggles the mind. Why would someone have her own sister killed?"

"I couldn't believe it myself at first, but I listened in on the interrogation and I heard the guy's testimony," Jon shares.

———

After the testimony of the suspected assassin, the detectives with the District Attorney's office conduct interviews with the members of the Bravo family and Athena's office staff to find out who may have a possible reason to hurt her. It is part of their job to check every lead. The suspected assassin already gave a description of the woman, and the police artist provides a drawing. They also order the suspected assassin to hand over the money paid to him by the woman to dust for fingerprints.

The police exercises discretion in their investigation since it is not your usual attempted murder case. There have been cases of persons wanting to have their siblings killed, but it is something they don't expect to see happen. They refuse to believe that people are capable of having their own flesh and blood eliminated for selfish reasons and out of jealousy, but they cannot discount the fact that it does happen in today's dysfunctional society.

They are extra careful in questioning Rodrigo and Marina, who are already emotionally affected by the incident as they expect parents to be. Detectives Russo and Stone visit their home to question them.

Mr. and Mrs. Bravo, do you know of anybody who may want to hurt your daughter?," Detective Russo inquires.

"No. She is a kind and gentle person. I can't imagine anyone would want to hurt her." Rodrigo replies.

"Would you know if she has enemies?," Detective Stone adds.

"Not to our knowledge. She has a number of friends, but no enemies," says Rodrigo.

"Does she get along with your other daughter?," Detective Russo probes.

"Are you suspecting Diana? She's not capable of doing such a thing," Marina quickly reacts.

"We're not suggesting anything, ma'am, but we have to ask questions. This is part of the investigation. We're just doing our job," Detective Russo elaborates. "We'll let you know of any developments in the investigation. Luckily your daughter didn't sustain serious injuries."

"Her guardian angel must have protected her. I dread to think what might have happened to her if that cyclist didn't knock down that assassin accidentally," Marina adds.

———

Athena's office staff are also questioned by the two detectives, and they say the same thing about her. They report that Athena is a likable person and their office loves her, so they cannot imagine that anybody would want to hurt her.

"Is there someone jealous of her perhaps? She's beautiful and successful," Detective Russo suggests.

"None that we know of," the writers concur.

CHAPTER 42

Precautions

"You can't stay in your condo at this time," Jon cautions Athena. "I'm concerned about your safety, so I insist you move to my condo temporarily. You can occupy the other room."

"Okay, Jon, if you say so. What happens now?"

"We'll leave it to the police to handle the investigation. I'll continue to follow it up myself."

⸺⁓•◦⟡◦⟡◦⟡◦•⁓⸺

Jon helps Athena move her things to his condo. He refuses to leave her by herself and cautions her to stay indoors at work.

"If I can help it, I don't want you out of my sight. I don't know what I'd do if something bad should happen to you," he reveals his fear. Athena is deeply touched by his concern. "How's the security in your office?"

"They're rather strict."

"Good, because we have to look into that too, plus all likely places where you can be a target."

"I'm sorry for getting you into this, Jon. It pains me to think that my own twin sister wants me out of the picture. I haven't done anything wrong to her."

"You're part of me now, so I'm involved in everything that concerns you. You'll soon be my wife. When this is over, we'll start planning our wedding, okay? You know, darling, this is a case of sibling rivalry. There are overt signs. You may not feel that you're competing with Diana, but she has a different view. She considers you a threat."

"To the extent of wanting me dead?" She shivers for a moment and seeks Jon's embrace.

"There may be something psychologically wrong with Diana. Such behavior isn't normal."

Jon constantly keeps an eye on Athena, and never leaves her alone. He cannot take any chances when it comes to her safety. Athena has never experienced being so cared for. She appreciates going home to Jon's condo because they have a longer "together" time and she is able to cook for him and attend to his needs, like looking after his clothes as her mom does for her dad. She likes to smell the clothes he has worn because they smell of him. Everyday they have breakfast together. Sometimes Jon insists on cooking breakfast for them.

He drops her off at work and waits until she is safely inside the building. She does not leave the office to go to lunch, except if it is with Jon. He believes they should take precautions while the investigation is still ongoing because they cannot foretell what may happen. Athena's life may still be in danger.

Jon controls their weekend schedule too. He reserves their Saturday mornings for Coalition on Homelessness.

They now rarely eat out, and instead Athena cooks for them. She enjoys cooking for Jon and sometimes try out new recipes for him. They watch movies and TV at home. Even if they have to go to the supermarket, Jon always stays beside her. They also have their "alone" time when they are in front of their laptops working from home or simply answering e-mail messages.

"Jon, this is like practicing for our husband and wife roles, except that we're not sleeping together."

"I'm comfortable with the setup. By the time this is over, we'd be experts in living together and keeping house. Then we only have the 'sleeping together' part to master and enjoy," he kids and glances naughtily at her, and she becomes self-conscious.

"Thanks for being a patient partner, Jon. I can't imagine myself spending my life with someone else. Have you noticed? We haven't had a major quarrel since we became steady."

"Consider that a good sign. That's because we're compatible, love. It took me a while to find the right woman until I met you."

Chapter 43

Accused

The police is compelled to include Diana in the line-up because of her strong resemblance to the artist's drawing. She does not refuse when the police invites her because she is certain that she has more credibility than the suspected assassin. There are seven women in the line-up, and the suspected assassin watches through the one-way mirror as they walk in holding a number and form a straight line facing forward. They all have short brown hair.

"We have seven women in the line-up. Take your time and look closely at each one of them," Detective Russo instructs Harry.

Harry does as he is told and scrutinizes the women one by one. He makes another pass and looks at each of them intently. He stops with Diana and focuses on her longer.

"She's No. 5."

"Are you very sure?"

"Positive. I can't forget that pretty face."

The fingerprint result also comes out, and it matches Diana's.

The detective reads Diana her Miranda rights while handcuffing her. She is fingerprinted, then locked up in jail. It is a very humiliating experience for someone with Diana's supercilious nature. What makes it even worse is that it gets reported in the local news. Her parents are devastated, and so is Paolo, who has no previous knowledge of the incident.

"I'll get Jon to handle your case," Paolo comforts her after rushing to the jail house.

"No, Paolo, you can't hire Jon because he's Athena's fiancé and he is surely her legal adviser."

"What? How come I don't know about this?" Paolo is nonplussed and gestures with his hands. "Nobody said anything about it. This comes as a complete surprise to me. Why didn't you tell me, Diana?"

"I'm sorry. I was just as shocked myself. When I learned that Jon is Athena's fiancé, I asked him why he didn't tell me or you. He said it's inappropriate for a lawyer to divulge his personal relationships to his client. He has a point, Paolo."

"Don't worry. I'll get you another lawyer. Diana, please understand that whatever you did, it won't change how I feel about you, *amore*. I'll get you out of this."

"Thank you, Paolo. I need you now more than ever."

———————

Jon is present during Diana's arraignment in court. The District Attorney presents her crime of hiring an assassin to kill her sister, which makes her equally guilty of attempted murder. The judge posts bail at $500,000 and schedules the hearing a week after. Paolo is also present in court, but Jon avoids him because it is already embarrassing seeing Diana accused in court, and he believes it is best this way since he does not know what to say to him.

—⁓⁓⋄⊙⋅⊙⊙⊙⋅⊙⋄⁓⁓—

Paolo settles the bail amount right away so that Diana does not have to remain in jail. After picking her up in jail, she asks him to bring her to her parents' home so she can talk to them, and leave her for an hour with them. It is a sad meeting with her distraught parents, and for the first time, she cried and expressed remorse for hurting them with her action. Rodrigo and Marina cannot recall witnessing Diana cry before.

"Dad, Mom, I'm very sorry for what I did," she tells them in between sobs.

"Diana, I don't know what came over you that made you do this to your own sister," Rodrigo scolds her. "It's vile and senseless. What did you hope to accomplish?"

"What if Athena died,? Do you hate her that much?," Marina asks.

"I don't know. I can't explain it." Her tears flowed in torrents. "I just didn't want her to be happy. She always gets the best things. I was jealous of her, and I wanted to even the score."

"Even the score? Killing her will not do that. That's vengeance for nothing, Diana. It's terribly wrong." Rodrigo is now mad.

"What you say is not true, dear. We treated you the same, and you happen to be as smart and lovely as she is," Marina adds. "We love you both and we are proud of you."

"I'm sorry, Mom." She continues to sob. "I'm sorry for the wrong that I did. I don't know what possessed me to want to see Athena dead. I was insanely jealous of her. I've hurt you too with my action."

"How do you feel now? Do you still want to hurt your sister?," Rodrigo questions her.

"No, Dad. I've learned my lesson. It made me think hard about the wrong that I did while I was in jail. I've hurt my family. The negative publicity was bad enough. I dragged you all into it. It was humiliating for me too. It was horrible being photographed and fingerprinted as a criminal."

"Now you know. What do you intend to do now?" Rodrigo calms down a bit.

"I want to ask for Athena's forgiveness. I hope she'll forgive me. I've hurt her deeply. I was consumed with jealousy when I learned that she's getting married to someone distinguished like Jonathan Prentiss. That was the final straw which led me to my action. Dad, Mom, that's not normal, is it?

"That's definitely not normal, Diana," Rodrigo responds.

"Dad, Mom, I need help. Will you help me?," she practically begs them.

"We're always here for you, Diana," Rodrigo assures her. "Do you want to see a therapist?"

"I think I need one, Dad, and I'm willing to stay in jail as my punishment."

"First, you should go to Athena and apologize to her. Can you do that?," Rodrigo inquires.

"I have to do it. I'll ask Paolo to accompany me. He's my pillar."

"Who's Paolo, dear?" Marina is curious.

"He's my boyfriend. I'll let you meet him when he comes for me later. He's a wonderful man, and he stayed by me the whole time. He paid my bail. I regret everything, and I blame myself for what I did. I don't know why I envied Athena for being engaged to Jonathan Prentiss when I have Paolo."

Chapter 44

Forgiveness

Rodrigo and Marina meet Paolo, and they like him. They observe that he is devoted to Diana and truly loves her despite her crime. They insist on being present when Diana apologizes to Athena, and Diana agrees because she knows she needs all the support, especially from family. Rodrigo offers to call Athena to tell her of their plan, and they set a date for the meeting.

"How do you feel about it? Are you prepared to face Diana?," Jon asks Athena, while cradling her in his arms.

"I guess I have to go through it. I'll feel safe with you and my parents present. What I need is her sincerity and genuine repentance. Despite what she did, I don't hate her. She's still my sister."

"You have a kind heart, Athena." He kisses her head. "I suppose she's sincere. She won't go to all this trouble if she's not. I'll be there next to you. Besides, you may need a lawyer," he kids her.

Jon has a way of lighting up Athena's mood even during a tense moment like the eventual confrontation.

He is always there for her, and she is thankful for his reliable presence.

———ᴧᴧᴧᴑᴏᴙᴑᴏᴙᴑᴏᴧᴧᴧ———

Jon reserves the conference room on the ground floor of his condo building for the meeting. Jon and Athena go down to the venue a few minutes before the appointed time. She is slightly nervous, and Jon holds her hand to calm her. Diana arrives with Paolo and their parents. After the usual greetings, they take their seats. Diana goes right to the point and faces her twin sister.

"Athena, I'm very sorry for the wrong that I did. I was driven by my jealousy of you. When Dad announced your engagement to Jon, I flipped. I couldn't believe you upstaged me again. I always felt you overshadowed me, that you surpassed me in everything. My mind was controlled by the belief that you are the better twin, and I fought against that."

"That's not true, Diana. Our parents treated us equally. We are both precious to them I'm aware how smart and talented you are, and I didn't even think that we were competing against each other. I have no intention of upstaging you nor putting one over you. Whatever I do is never about you. You're exceptional in your own field. I don't look at it as some sort of a contest between us, and I never think that I'm better than you either. Believe me."

"Really? That's how you feel? I'm glad to hear this. All these years I treated you as an enemy, and you took it silently and did not retaliate. I was mean to you, and I'm sorry for that. Do you hate me for what I did to you?"

"No, I don't. You're my twin sister and we will always be part of each other no matter what happens. When you were mean to me in the past, I just avoided you. It was easier that way."

"I deeply regret what I did, and I'm willing to face the consequences. I told our parents that I want to undergo psychological therapy. What is important to me now is your forgiveness. My apology extends to all the bad things I did in the past, and I know there have been many. Will you forgive me, Athena, after all that I had done to you?"

"Yes, I forgive you. Let's forget the past. No ill feelings from now on, okay?"

"Okay. Thank you for your understanding." Diana rises and goes to Athena to hug her.

"At last, after all these years," Rodrigo mutters, referring to the long animosity between their twins.

The prevailing tension is dispersed. Rodrigo and Marina approach their daughters and join in the group hug, with Marina in tears. Jon and Paolo shake hands.

"Does that make us brothers-in-law?," Paolo says to Jon.

"I'm not sure about relationship labels, but it certainly means that we're both part now of the Bravo family, Paolo."

CHAPTER 45

Plans

"Jon, how does the law go? I had forgiven Diana, so does that free her of her crime?," Athena asks.

"I'll take care of that. I'll talk to the District Attorney and tell him that you're not filing a case of attempted murder against Diana. In such a case, usually they'll not pursue it, considering they have more serious crime concerns."

"Thank you, Jon. I'd like to put this behind us."

———————

The District Attorney sees no point in pursuing the case against Diana after Jon told him of the reconciliation. Diana's case does not reach the court anymore.

———————

Paolo invites the Bravo family, including Jon and Athena, to *Paolo's* for dinner to celebrate Diana's freedom. Rodrigo and Marina are delighted to meet Luigi, who sits behaved next to his father. Secretly, Paolo treats the occasion as an opportunity to propose to Diana, but she does not know about it. When they are all seated in the private room he reserved, Paolo takes out an engagement ring and goes down on one knee in front of a surprised Diana.

"Diana, my goddess, will you marry me?"

Diana is caught totally unaware, but she responds without any hesitation.

"Yes, Paolo, I will marry you." They kiss and hug.

"Mr. Bravo, may I ask for Diana's hand in marriage?," Paolo asks Rodrigo.

"Yes, Paolo. You have my blessing."

Paolo slips the ring into Diana's finger, and they all clap. Luigi also claps his hands and approaches Paolo and Diana to hug them. "I want to be at the wedding, Papa."

"Of course, Luigi. You will carry the rings, won't you?"

"Cool!"

"He learned that expression in school. All the kids use it," Paolo explains with a smile.

"So, Paulo, this dinner is not exactly to celebrate my freedom as you say, but you were really going to propose to me?," Diana questions him.

"It can be both, *amore*. You see, I didn't want you to suspect anything." His statement is followed by an amused reaction from the family.

"Imagine, I'm marrying a chef, and I don't have any talent in the kitchen."

"That's all right. Cooking is my passion, and I'll take care of the kitchen. Besides, you have other talents," Paolo hints mischievously.

From across the table, Diana glances at Athena and catches her eye.

"Thank you," Diana says.

"What for?"

"For not pursuing the case against me."

"I wasn't planning to. Congratulations on your engagement."

"I haven't congratulated you on yours," and they smile at each other.

"I'm now seeing a therapist," Diana admits.

"I'm glad for you."

"Jon is a fine and handsome man and obviously head over heels with you. You deserve him, Athena."

"I'm madly in love with him too. Look at your Paolo. He's quite a guy, very good-looking, and he's crazy about you."

"I can't believe we're getting married to two great handsome guys," Diana quips.

The family has a joyous time, and enjoy the Italian food served at *Paolo's*. Luigi gets his favorite *bolognese* pasta. Rodrigo and Marina are ecstatic about the recent developments in their twins' lives. There is the unexpected reconciliation, then two weddings to anticipate.

"When are you two planning to get married?," Jon asks Paolo and Diana.

"Right after your wedding," Paolo answers. "Your announcement came first, so you go ahead. We'll have our wedding in Tuscany, where my parents and family are. I have a large family."

"So it's going to be a big lively event then," Athena predicts.

"You can bet on that," Paolo answers. "Italian weddings usually are."

"I'm already excited," Diana admits.

"That means then that we won't be at your wedding since by that time we'll be on our honeymoon," Jon comments and looks at Athena lovingly.

"We can give Dad and Mom free plane tickets so they can be there for the wedding," Diana shares.

"That's great. It will be quite an experience for them. They've never been to Europe," Athena adds.

CHAPTER 46

Social Network

Athena learns from Jon that his group composed of lawyers like him has a Friday night-out. There are five of them in the group working in different firms, and all Harvard Law School graduates.

"I've heard of 'night-out with the boys' from married friends. That's the term, isn't it? You never mentioned it before," Athena notes.

"That's because we haven't had one recently. The wife of one of the guys had a baby, and another one was away on a trip, plus other reasons in between. We have it only when we're all available so no one misses out on the news and updates. It's more fun when we're complete," Jon clarifies.

"What happens during one of those nights?"

"Oh, the usual. We talk mostly about our cases and updates on our lives. We speak Legalese, which is understandable to all of us. Of course, we eat and drink beer, but try to stay sober. The food is good there."

"Legalese, huh? That puts me out of place. It must be fun for you guys."

"Clean fun, no hanky-panky. There's one place we frequent – Reggie's Bar. We have a room reserved there. I'm telling you this because we'll have one this coming Friday after some absence."

"Thanks for letting me know. We have no plans between the two of us, so have a nice time with your friends."

"You'll meet all of them soon. David is the one whose wife just had a baby, their first. Caleb has two kids, and Bruce and Kumar are single. Kumar is Indian. We were schoolmates at Harvard."

"I guess it's different with us women. My friends and Barbara's from College don't see each other on a regular basis, but we meet for lunch occasionally. I go out with my officemates and the writers in my unit once in a while, usually to celebrate a birthday."

———

Jon's lawyer group has its usual night-out at Reggie's Bar. They had not seen each other for some time, so the updates are longer. Jon starts by telling the four guys that he's getting married, and his announcement is met with cheers. He passes Athena's photo around which meets the guys' approval. David invites all of them to the christening of his new baby boy.

"Jon, will you be his godfather?," he asks.

"Of course, David. What will you name him?"

"He'll be my junior. We're not sure we'll have more since my wife had a difficult delivery."

"May I bring my fiancée to the christening?"

"Sure. We all want to meet her. So, Jon, you finally found the right one, huh? I'm glad for you. Hey, guys, don't forget the date. Caleb, bring your wife too. The christening will be Saturday after next at St. Patrick Church at 11:00 a.m., followed by lunch.

The guys usually have beer and assorted nuts first while they chat and update each other. They have dinner afterwards of ribs or steak, which are Reggie's specialties.

"Hey, Bruce, tell us about your recent trip," Caleb pipes in.

"Where did you go?," Kumar asks.

"I was in Turkey for two weeks. It was my vacation time, and a friend of mine who lives there urged me to visit him. Turkey is a beautiful place. You should all go there. What I enjoyed most is Pamukkale, which is situated in the inner Aegean region. These are several graduated natural pools. I have photos in my iPad. Take a look at them." Bruce passes his iPad around for the guys to see.

"This is amazing, Bruce. I'd like to see this myself," Kumar wishes.

"Isn't Cappadocia also in Turkey?," Caleb asks Bruce.

"Right. It's an interesting place and rich in history."

———————

Jon stands as godfather to David's son during the christening. Athena finally meets his friends and their wives. She notices the strong rapport among Jon's Harvard friends. They obviously enjoy each other's company. *And I'm sure they speak Legalese among themselves,* she concludes.

CHAPTER 47

Jon Turns 30

Athena is aware that it is going to be Jon's 30th birthday soon. She wants to throw him a surprise party, but she is not sure how to go about it to ensure that he will not find out. She requests Amanda's help since she handles Jon's schedule and knows his friends and contacts.

She is in the thick of preparations for their wedding, but Jon is the most special person in her life. Turning 30 is an important milestone for him, so she feels she should devote some time to plan a birthday surprise for the love of her life.

"I want him to be really surprised and not suspect anything," she admits to Amanda. "This is what I'll do. I'll tell him I'm treating him to dinner on his birthday. Everybody should be at the restaurant at least 15 minutes early so Jon will not spot any of the guests arriving. Then we'll arrive at the venue together. Amanda, I'll need you there to manage the guests in the room. When you get your warning, everybody should be quiet."

"No problem. I can talk to the *maître d'* to cooperate with us and signal me as soon as you arrive."

"You can also help me with the guest list. Aside from Mr. Blake and Mr. Johnson, you know whom to invite among his colleagues in the office. I'll draw up a guest list of my own. We'll include his friends from Harvard. When we invite the guests, we should warn them not to say a word of it to Jon, or else that will spoil everything."

"Don't worry. I'll make sure it's kept a secret until the last moment. Don't you feel excited? I'd like to catch JP's expression when we surprise him."

"I'm excited, but I'm also nervous that it won't turn out as planned. Can you order the cake? I'll take care of the menu and talk to the chef. Maybe he can give me suggestions for the menu. Should we have a streamer?"

"Why not? I can order that too."

"Okay. I guess we have everything covered. It has to be by word of mouth, so we won't issue invitations anymore to keep it really secret. We'll work out the seating arrangement and nameplates when we have all the names of the guests."

Athena's guest list contains 25 people, including wives. Aside from the two senior partners, Amanda submits three more names from Jon's office. Athena includes Rodrigo and Marina, Paolo and Diana, and Angelo and Barbara. Earlier, she made reservations at the Marriott Marquis.

On the morning of Jon's birthday, Athena calls to greet him.

"Happy Birthday, Jon. How's the birthday boy feeling today?"

"Just great, darling. Thank you. I'm looking forward to your treat tonight. You said to come in coat and tie? I hope this is not too much trouble for you."

"No trouble at all. It's just dinner, Jon. I want to spend a special time with you on your birthday. I'll give you your birthday gift later."

"Oh, I have a gift? I'll pick you up at 7:00, love. See you later."

Athena got him a pair of cuff links engraved with "JP". Jon gets successive calls from his mom and siblings during the day to greet him a Happy Birthday.

⎯⎯ ᴡᴡᴄᴏᴇᴛᴏᴏᴛᴇᴏᴏᴡᴡ ⎯⎯

Athena wears a knee-length electric blue shift dress for the dinner. Jon is punctual as usual. She greets and kisses him as she gets into his car and hands him his gift. He is his vibrant self.

"Thanks for the gift. I'll open it later. My fiancée is treating me to dinner. What more can I wish for on my birthday?"

"I just want to please you on your birthday, darling"

"Did you just call me 'darling'?" He cocks his head to one side and glances at her.

"I guess I did," she answers shyly.

He slows down and stops the car by the side of the road, then draws her to him and kisses her wildly. "Thanks for that."

"Golly, Jon, I should call you that if I want to be kissed savagely." She fans herself with her hand, her heart beating fast after that kiss, and Jon is evidently amused.

When they reach the restaurant, he helps her out of the car. She notes that he is wearing a dark suit which fits him perfectly. *He always looks dashing in a suit.*

"Lead the way, my love," he kids her.

Athena cannot help but be nervous that something may go wrong for Jon to suspect. They walk holding hands with Athena actually leading.

"You got a private room?," he inquires as they stop in front of a door.

"The best for you, Jon."

She lets him open the door for her. It all seems so quiet. As he opens the door, the guests inside burst into a chorus of "Surprise!" Jon is dumb-founded and speechless for a few seconds. He keeps shaking his head and smiling at the guests. Then he turns to Athena.

"You tricked me!," he blurts out within earshot in an accusatory tone, but with still a smile on his face.

"Happy 30th Birthday, Jon." She hugs him.

The guests approach one by one to greet Jon, and he shakes the hands of the men and gives the ladies a peck in the cheek. He is glad to see Blake and Johnson, his office colleagues, his friends, and Athena's family.

"I never expected anything like this," he confesses to the guests. "Thank you for celebrating my birthday with me. This is my best birthday ever. I can't believe you're all in on this."

The revelry lasted for several hours, with Jon enjoying himself eating, drinking, and interacting with the people close to him. Towards the tail end of the surprise dinner, he turns to Athena.

"Thank you, darling. I can't believe you maneuvered this without my knowing it. I didn't even suspect you were up to something. You made my turning 30 just great."

"You should thank Amanda too. She was part of the conspiracy."

CHAPTER 48

Preparations

Athena and Diana are both deep into their wedding plans. Diana's only concern is her wedding dress since most of the preparations will be done in Tuscany. It is a different story for Athena, whose wedding will be in San Francisco. Marina helps her with the initial preparations, but they hire a wedding planner to free them of the headaches, which normally accompany an affair of such nature.

The twins' varied tastes are evident in their choice of a wedding dress. Diana's design choice is simple but sexy. She opts for a body-fitting bustier with the accent on the delicate lace veil. Athena prefers a dainty creation which has a see-through lacy effect along the bodice and short sleeves with a bouffant skirt. The members of Diana's wedding entourage are all from Tuscany, except Luigi.

Athena is caught in a whirl of parties before her wedding. She is feted at three bridal showers by Diana, Barbara, and her officemates. She asks Diana to be her maid of honor. After their reconciliation, she feels that her twin should have a major role in her wedding. Barbara is bridesmaid. Marianne's daughter is the flower girl, and Robert's son is the ring bearer. She wants to keep her entourage at a minimum. Robert is Jon's best man.

Athena told Jon earlier that she does not want a big and expensive wedding. So they are planning for a conservative and medium-size wedding where they can invite their families and close friends. It takes a couple of weeks for Jon and Athena to sit down and discuss their wedding, and how they envision it to be. They agree on almost all aspects.

<center>~~~~∽∽∽∾∾∿◦⊙❋⊙◦∿∾∾∽∽~~~~</center>

For his part, Jon disagrees with his friends about their plan of organizing a bachelor's party for him.

"Oh, no. No bachelor's party."

"What's your reason, Jon?," Caleb inquires.

"I've been to a lot of them, and I don't approve of what happens during one."

"What part of it don't you approve of?," Bruce asks him.

"Guys, the idea behind a bachelor's party is to give the prospective groom a last fling before he gives up his bachelorhood, right?"

"What's your objection to that, Jon?," David counters.

"Remember your bachelor's party, David? That sexy girl in a bikini practically seduced you. By the way, did your wife know about that?"

"Well, unfortunately, she found out because she accidentally saw the photos, and we had a big fight before the wedding, but we patched things up later when I convinced her it was nothing serious."

"That's what I mean, guys. I don't want to start my marriage on the wrong footing. Maybe you think it wasn't serious, David, but the girl didn't think so. She seemed bent on seducing you that night, and she could have succeeded if I didn't divert your attention. You were already drunk and could easily have succumbed to such temptation. Those women are hired for that, and they are conscious of it. Besides, she must have been wishing she could spend the night with a good-looking guy like you."

"I see your point, Jon. I don't think I'd want one too when I get married. I'm Indian, and my family happens to be quite conservative," Kumar offers his side. "They'll never be able to understand such a ritual."

"So what are we going to do for Jon then before he loses his single status?," Caleb addresses the group.

"Guys, why don't we just go out for dinner, just the five of us, and enjoy each other's company? We can have a rollicking time too," Jon suggests.

"Not a bad idea," Bruce agrees, and the other guys approve the suggestion.

Epilogue

The day of the wedding arrives. Athena wakes up to a glorious day. She is wrapped in anticipation of her big day. She knows that Jon had his dinner with the Harvard guys the night before. She would like him to tell her about it, but she's following the rule of not seeing or even talking to her groom on the day of the wedding. *I miss Jon already.* She cannot describe her excitement. *So this is how the bride feels before her wedding, all jitters.* She reads through her vows, which she will recite to Jon, and does a bit of editing.

Jon gets out of bed grinning. *It's my wedding day, and at last my beloved Athena is going to be my wife.* After preparing himself a heavy breakfast of omelette, hash browns, rolls, and coffee, he also goes through his vows. He wants to be sure he has written everything that is in his heart.

His mom, his siblings, and their families arrived two days before the wedding, and are staying at the hotel. He brought along Athena to meet his family and took them to lunch upon their arrival. Then he gave them a tour of San Francisco in a van he hired for them. Although they have been there before, there were places they wanted to visit with the kids.

Towards afternoon of the wedding day, the lady hairdresser arrives at Athena's condo to work on her hair, which she wears brushed up in a bun held by a round band encrusted with *faux* rhinestones and pearl where her long veil hangs from behind it. She is the epitome of a blushing bride even if she is wearing just light make-up, which she insists on applying on herself. Her mom goes to her condo to help her get ready for her late afternoon wedding at St. Ignatius Church. Marina helps her put on her gown. She goes to the full-length mirror and admires the woman that looks back at her. She stares at the image of a radiant bride with joy etched on her lovely face. She makes sure that she is not late for her wedding because her groom is a very punctual person. She also does not believe in the saying that "*the bride is always late.*"

As the bridal car arrives at the church entrance ten minutes early, Rodrigo takes Athena's hand to guide her for their walk to the altar. They allow the entourage dressed in attractive champagne-hued gowns to proceed first, keeping a reasonable distance. When the time comes for their walk, Athena is all nervousness, holding on tightly to her father's arm with her bouquet on her other hand. She looks towards the altar and casts a glance at Jon standing there, smiling at her. *He looks very handsome in his tuxedo.* All eyes are on the bride with a look of admiration as she takes her slow walk with her father along the aisle. Their faces are just a blur to Athena at the moment.

Jon receives her from Rodrigo and smiles down at her as he takes her hand and squeezes it, and it calms her down somehow. She knows it is his way of comforting her. The officiating priest is Fr. Francis Gregory, S.J., who is Jon's good friend and spiritual adviser. Before Fr. Gregory starts the ceremony, Jon whispers to his bride-to-be, "You're very beautiful," and she mouths back a 'thank you'. After Jonathan Adam Prentiss and Athena Mary Bravo pledge their I-dos, Fr. Gregory reserves some moments for them to recite their vows to each other. They face each other, holding both hands.

Jon: "Athena, my love, the first time I met you, you immediately captured my heart with your total personality. Although being an intelligent person you personify the goddess you were named after, you're more than that to me. How you look on the outside transcends physical attributes because behind that beautiful façade is a kind and loving person I've learned to love deeply. You are the woman I've been waiting for all my life. I'm always happy being with you, and I love you with all my heart. I promise to be faithful to you, and I say this in front of our families and all our guests, who are my witnesses (a murmur of amusement comes from inside the church). I'll take care of you, and I'll be the perfect partner to you. I don't believe I can love anybody as much as I love you. Sorry, Mom (he looks and smiles at his mom, and the crowd continues to be amused). This is the happiest day of my life, that you'll finally be my wife, and we'll start to build and share a life together, then eventually raise a family of our own. Darling, I love you very much, and that is one thing that will never change."

Athena: "I love you too very much, Jon. I've never met anyone like you. 'Wonderful' is too mild a word to describe you. You're brilliant and good-looking, but despite your good looks, there isn't a trace of arrogance in you. I confess that I love your English accent since I first heard you speak because you sounded like my favorite character, James Bond (an amused murmur ensues from the guests). You're my hero now. After knowing you well, I can't imagine living a life without you. You're also my rock, Jon. You're always there for me, and you comfort me. I see the world and people differently and positively now because of you. You are a person with a soul, and your goodness knows no bounds. I learned this from you, and I marvel at the kindness that springs from your heart. I thank your late father and your mother, who is present here now, for the kind of person you are. Jon, darling (he smiles at the way she is addressing him), I look forward with much excitement to our life together, and our wedding is just the beginning. Remember that I will always love you."

The church crowd is touched by the vows Jon and Athena recited to each other. Some are teary-eyed, particularly Marina and Jon's Mom. When Fr. Gregory announces, "Jon, you may now kiss the bride," Jon immediately draws Athena into his arms and kisses her. The kiss takes so long that his Harvard friends call out to him, "That's enough, Jon," to the amusement of the guests.

"Now you're officially Mrs. Prentiss," he whispers to his happy bride.

It is a lovely and fun evening with everyone enjoying the reception and taking to the dance floor. Then the musicians play *"The Way You Look Tonight"* for the new couple. Jon and Athena dance to it and have eyes only for each other. Later Jon also asks his mom, his mother-in-law, and his sister to dance with him one after the other, and even his niece, Marianne's daughter. Athena gets to dance with her dad too.

After saying their goodbyes, they take a late flight to Montecarlo, Jon's choice for their month-long honeymoon. They slept through most of the 13-hour flight to get some needed rest.

The honeymoon proves to be beyond Athena's expectations. Their hotel room in Montecarlo has a spectacular, breath-taking view.

"Thank you for saving yourself for me," Jon tells her afterwards.

"It was worth it, Jon."

"How do you feel now, Mrs. Prentiss?"

"Deliriously happy."

"Do you like being married to me?"

"Yes, very much. It's heaven."

End

About the Author

Cristina Monro is a penname the author uses when writing fiction. The author is a Filipino who shuttles between the Philippines and Singapore. She is an editor, writer, and English instructor. She has a post-graduate Diploma in Language and Literacy Education from the University of the Philippines, and a Bachelor of Arts degree, major in English, from Xavier University. She earned a Certificate for Teaching English as a Second/Foreign Language from De La Salle University. She also completed the Program for Development Managers at the Asian Institute of Management and the Secretarial course at Maryknoll College.

She earlier received a Fellowship Grant from the US-Asia Environmental Partnership and observed the environmental programs of the US and Canada. In the Philippines, she worked for a number of years with San Miguel Corporation, Pilipinas Shell, and Accenture Philippines as Editor, and received several awards from the Public Relations Society of the Philippines in recognition of her work.

She is an author of three published books and co-authored a textbook on Communication Arts. Her hobbies include oil painting of landscapes and still life, mosaic art, patchwork quilting, embroidery, playing the piano and the guitar, and solving crossword puzzles.